Opening the gate Mory held out the apple. The pony put its teeth around it and pulled. Mory held tight to the bottom half and the apple split. The pony ate and Mory, her heart pounding, slipped the twine around its neck. The pony, quite unconcerned, nuzzled her hand for the rest of the apple.

"Have you come to be mine? Have you?" she said gently. The pony pushed at her with its muzzle. Mory pulled on the twine and the pony moved forward. Thrilled at her success, she led the pony into the yard and headed for the paddock at the back of the house.

by Elizabeth Lindsay
illlustrated by Linda Boddy

Scholastic Children's Books,
Scholastic Publications Ltd,
7-9 Pratt Street, London NW1 0AE, UK

Scholastic Inc.,
730 Broadway, New York, NY 10003, USA

Scholastic Canada Ltd,
123 Newkirk Road, Richmond Hill,
Ontario, Canada L4C 3G5

Ashton Scholastic Pty Ltd,
P O Box 579, Gosford, New South Wales,
Australia

Ashton Scholastic Ltd,
Private Bag 1, Penrose, Auckland,
New Zealand

First published by Scholastic Publications Ltd, 1993

0 590 55136 1

Typeset by A J Latham, Dunstable
Printed by Cox & Wyman Ltd, Reading, Berks

10 9 8 7 6 5 4 3 2 1

Contents

1 We Shouldn't Have Come 1
2 A New Beginning 15
3 Night Visitor 25
4 Midnight Dancer 37
5 Enquiries 48
6 Which Way To Turn 59
7 Preparations 71
8 The Pony Sales 82
9 Despair 95
10 The Lesson 108
11 Into The Hills 119
12 The Rescue 130
13 Birthday Surprise 140

For Hannah

ONE

We Shouldn't Have Come

Rain lashed the windscreen. The dull sound of the engine and the beat of the wipers gave a rhythm to the words repeating themselves in Mory's head over and over: Croeso y Cymru. Croeso y Cymru. The words on the sign meant Welcome to Wales. She tried to stop them, but new words took their place: I don't want to go. I don't want to go. She had begged. She had pleaded.

The car bumped along a rutted lane. Mory sat hunched, her arms around the cat basket. Why did children always have to do what grown-ups wanted? Josh looked up from his joke book. If he told another joke she would scream. Fortunately he didn't – he looked out of the window. There was still nothing to see except mist and hedgerows. Splodge mewed long and loud from the confines of his cat basket.

"Nearly there," her father announced from the passenger seat in the front. Her mother was driving the last lap of the journey which had begun on a sunny morning in Surrey and was ending in a wet afternoon in Wales.

"David, don't let me miss the turning." Sheila peered past the swoosh, swoosh of the wipers into the mist that wrapped around them.

"There it is!"

"Blast!"

Sheila backed the car and turned between the posts of an open gate. A peeling sign announced Llangabby Farm.

"I hope the removal lorry gets here soon," said David, folding up the map and stuffing it into the holder on the car door. "Well driven, love."

"Yes, well done, Mum," said Josh from the back.

Mory maintained a stony silence. She couldn't see anything well done about it. She'd been driven from her home and her friends to what looked like a dump. She was morose and angry. For weeks she'd been dreading it and now it had happened. It had been no good Mum saying it was a great adventure and Dad saying it was now or never – they'd ruined everything. She'd just been made captain of the Waring School table tennis team, the best thing that had ever happened to her. It was all very well them saying they'd buy her a table tennis table for her birthday. It was pointless if she had no one to play with. And what about Hannah, her best friend? Tears pricked her eyes as she thought about saying goodbye. They had both cried.

The car stopped in front of a grey stone house. A woman, with a green mac and hood draped over her head and shoulders like a cape, came down the steps from the house. Mory wanted to stay sitting in the car for ever but the woman opened the door. She and the rest of the Harper family climbed stiffly out and Mory suffered herself to be kissed and hugged. This was her aunt, Olwen Morgan, her father's sister.

"Went back to her roots," her father had said when he described Olwen. Mory had only met her once before.

"Is that the cat?" asked her aunt, tapping the top of the basket which Mory held.

"It's Splodge," said Mory.

"He'll have to be locked up until he gets used to the place," said Aunt Olwen.

"Leave him in the car for now," said her father. "He'll be quite safe." Mory placed Splodge's basket on the back seat. As soon as this was done she found herself ushered up the front steps.

The two families hadn't kept up and now they were to be living next door to one another. Grown-ups make you sick, thought Mory as she peered along the dark, panelled hall. You never knew what they were going to do next. I suppose Dad thinks we're going back to our roots. Mory felt her roots to be in Surrey, at Waring where she'd grown up. She felt pulled up like a weed. Sympathy for plants overwhelmed her. How horrible to be a dandelion!

At the end of the hallway was a large room which turned out to be the kitchen. A girl of roughly Mory's age stood by the long table. Mory knew her from her photograph. It was Cara, her cousin. Cara smiled shyly and Mory returned a rude stare. Cara looked away, blushing.

"Come along, Cara," said Aunt Olwen, bustling in. "Pop the kettle on, there's a dear. We'll have a nice cup of tea. You'll need reviving after your long journey. Sit down. Sit down now."

The Harper family arranged themselves around the table.

"We mustn't stay long, Olwen," said Dad. "We must be there to help the removal men unload." Olwen paused in her bustle.

"Bad news, I'm afraid. The lorry broke down on the motorway. They rang to say they wouldn't arrive until tomorrow. But don't worry – you can stay here tonight and we'll all help in the morning." Olwen put a plate of scones on the table and Cara followed with a plate of biscuits. "You look exhausted as it is. It's a blessing in disguise if you ask me. Gives you time for a breather." Mum smiled.

"Thanks, Olwen. You're probably right."

Dad looked disgruntled but there was nothing he could do.

"Well, at least we can see the place and work out where everything is to go," said Mum.

"What about Splodge?" asked Mory.

"Cara'll make him comfortable in a stable. He'll be fine there until he gets used to the place."

"But he always sleeps on my bed."

"Well," said Aunt Olwen doubtfully, "we don't usually have animals in the house."

"The stable'll be fine," said David.

"Dad!"

"That's enough, Mory. You can't expect other people to break their rules for you."

"He'll be fine in the stable," Cara said. "You needn't worry about him."

"He'll be lonely,' said Mory.

"You can visit him," said Sheila, and that was that. Mory felt rotten. Three scones and four biscuits later she felt a lot better. Not that she counted but Josh did.

"You'll get fat as a pig if you go on like that," he said, grinning. Mory ignored him.

In spite of everything Mory warmed to Aunt Olwen. The kitchen began to interest her too. It was old fashioned. There was a double ceramic sink with wooden drainers. The cooker was a huge affair that sat in the large fireplace. It had big lids covering hot plates. It was on all the time and explained why the kitchen was so warm and cosy. It wasn't that there weren't modern things – there was a fridge and dishwasher. Will we have a big stove and a dishwasher in our house? Mory wondered. She caught her mother looking at her and turned away.

"Cara," said Aunt Olwen, "why don't you take Mory and Josh and show them where to put the cat? Sort them out some wellies and waterproofs. Introduce them to the farm."

Josh looked enthusiastic. Traipsing around in the mud and the muck was the last thing Mory wanted to do, but she did want to settle Splodge in the stable, which she imagined to be a cold, damp place. When Cara led her into it she was pleasantly surprised. It smelt sweet and had a warm bed of straw. Mory put the cat basket down and lifted the lid. Splodge, his eyes big and startled, looked out.

"He's lovely," said Cara. "I can see why you called him Splodge." Everyone could when they saw the large white patch on Splodge's face. "You can leave the basket. He can sleep in it. It'll make him feel safer."

Mory resented being told what to do. She ignored Cara and put some cat food and some water down in the corner.

"Who wants to look round the farm?" Cara asked.

"I do," said Josh.

"I'll stay with Splodge," said Mory, not looking up. The two of them went out, shutting the bottom half of the stable door. Mory felt abandoned. She watched Josh leap puddles as he followed Cara across the farmyard.

When they had gone there was nothing left to watch except the rain. The mist obliterated the view. Water dripped from the guttering above and splashed on to the mud below. Everything was sodden and sad.

Mory gave Splodge one last stroke. His back sank under her hand and he moved away. He wanted to explore his new home. With a sigh, Mory took the hint and let herself out, closing top and bottom stable door behind her.

What an awful place this is! she thought. Mory longed for home, but home didn't exist any more. It belonged to someone else now. Another person would be sleeping in her room. Her belongings were all bundled in a lorry, goodness knows where. This was to be home. She couldn't bear the thought.

Without meaning to she walked towards the yard entrance. The gates were open and led straight into a rutted track which ran along a steep hillside. Mory looked up. Raindrops smacked her face and she would have turned away but something caught her eye. A black pony! It was looking down at her through the mist, ears pricked attentively. They stared at one another until the whole world became the two of them. Everything was forgotten – the move, the rain, her lost friends.

"Hello," said Mory, breaking the spell without meaning to.

The pony snorted. It spun into the mist and was gone. She nearly yelled for it to come back but she knew it wouldn't. She stared at the place where it had been until her eyes stung.

Walking back to the farm house, Mory saw a black and white dog slink into an outbuilding. Shivering, she hurried indoors to the warmth of the kitchen and the company of her family.

"There's a black and white dog outside," Mory

told Aunt Olwen. "It's soaking wet." She didn't mention the pony. That was her secret.

"That's Mab back. They must have finished with the sheep. Glyn'll be in soon to say hello."

Olwen put the kettle on the stove ready to make her husband a fresh cup of tea. Mory wanted to lift the hot plate lid to feel what it was like, but was too shy to ask.

"We've got you in a ton of coal at Black Rock and I lit the stove this morning to make it a bit more cheerful for your arrival," said Olwen. "That house is going to need a fair bit doing to it, but then you know that."

The name Black Rock sounded grim. Thank goodness it's got a stove, thought Mory. At least it'll be warm.

"It's all hands to the grindstone," said David. "We've got a lot of work to cram into the Easter holidays."

"What a way to spend them!" groaned Mory to herself. "Decorating."

"The weather's broken badly," Aunt Olwen was saying. "It was fine until the day before yesterday. Since then it's done nothing but rain. But there you are – we're never satisfied." A door opened beyond the kitchen. "Here's Glyn."

Mory could hear voices through the kitchen door. Josh and Cara were coming in too. There was a lot of chatter as they took their boots off in the utility room beyond. A stocky man with bristling hair and a windblown face entered and beamed a welcome.

"Hello, David!" he cried. Dad rose to greet him and found his hand gripped tightly in a welcoming handshake.

"Hello, Sheila!" Uncle Glyn kissed Mum on the cheek. "It's good to see you."

"Couldn't you have done something about the weather?" Mum asked.

"I did. I ordered it 'specially. Typical Welsh weather," said Glyn.

"Don't say that. They'll think it's always like this," said Olwen.

"And you must be Morag," said Uncle Glyn, addressing Mory. She winced at the sound of her full name. "Hello to you." Uncle Glyn took her by both shoulders and planted a kiss on her cheek. "I met Josh out in the yard. Enjoying himself he was, sitting on the tractor." Josh rushed to join them.

"Uncle Glyn says I can drive it!"

"Only under my supervision, you understand, young man. Tractors are powerful and dangerous machines. And strictly speaking no one your age is allowed to drive one."

"You hear that, Josh?" said Dad. "Don't get any ideas about taking it off on your own."

"I won't. Of course I won't," said Josh. He crossed the kitchen and sat by Mory. "Cara's got a really nice pony called Misty. She's going to teach me to ride it."

"Bully for you!" said Mory unkindly.

"Are you coming, you two?" Mum said. "Uncle Glyn's offered to drive us to Black Rock Farm so we can take a look." Josh leaped to his feet.

"S'pose so," said Mory.

Uncle Glyn drove the Landrover out onto the steep rutted track. Mory looked up to where she had seen the black pony. Peering out of the back window she kept her eyes on the spot until it was lost in the mist, then she concentrated on holding on as the Landrover bumped and lurched down the track.

"I thought you said we were next door to Llangabby Farm," she grumbled to Mum, who was sitting next to her. "This is miles away."

"We are next door. People don't live so close together in the country."

"You're telling me!"

At last the Landrover stopped outside a grey stone house, smaller, yet similar to Llangabby Farm. It nestled closely into the side of the hill. There was an entrance to one side of the house, then outbuildings.

"The yard's round the back," said Uncle Glyn. The outbuildings were built of stone with grey slate roofs the same as the house. Mory couldn't

help thinking there was something pleasing in such solid buildings. They seemed to grow out of the land as if part of it, blending with the wildness of the hill into which they nestled.

"Now's our chance," said Mum. "It's stopped raining." So it had. The mist had lifted and they were no longer in the clouds. For a moment there was a patch of blue in the sky. The sun shone through, letting bright rays fall on the farm.

Mory watched entranced as wet slate and grey stone glinted in the light. But as suddenly as it had come it was gone, and without the sunshine everything felt sad again.

Uncle Glyn opened the front door.

"Welcome to Black Rock," he said. "Your new home. I hope you'll be very happy here." Mory stepped inside. It smelt.

"It's a little damp," said Uncle Glyn. "Not been lived in for a while, you see." Wallpaper peeled from the walls, the ceilings flaked and had great cracks across them. The paintwork, a gaudy orange and blue, clashed horribly.

"Old Charlie Jones was colour blind, you know, and as short-sighted as they come," said Glyn by way of explanation. Mory's spirits sank. It really was a dump, worse than her worst imaginings.

The room that was to be hers was at the top of the house. It was depressingly bare. The door was painted purple and the walls were covered with faded beige wallpaper.

"There's a nice dormer window in here," Uncle Glyn was saying, "and the one thing about Charlie was that he was always painting so nothing ever went rotten." The floor was bare. Their footsteps echoed on the floorboards. The room, like the whole house, was filthy.

Mory was overwhelmed by another wave of homesickness.

"We shouldn't have come!" she cried. "It's horrible." She burst into tears.

"Now, now, Mory," Uncle Glyn said. "A clean-up and a lick of new paint will work wonders." Sheila put her arms around her wretched daughter.

"I know how you feel, love. It's a big wrench. But Glyn's right – we'll soon make it home."

"We shouldn't have come," sobbed Mory. "I want to go home."

In the end they left her alone and went to look around the rest of the house. Mory cried until she couldn't cry any more. Outside it had begun to rain again. The drops beat against the window and streaked down the pane. She stared at the wet until Mum came and gave her another cuddle. Mory leaned her head against her mother's shoulder.

"Just now we're all feeling a bit like you, wondering what on earth we've let ourselves in for. But we know what we've got to do and we'll work hard to do it. We're going back with Glyn now. It won't seem so bad in the morning. Really it won't," said Mum.

Mory wondered if she dared believe her. Without knowing why she broke from her mother and went to the window. She pushed it open and leaned out. In the distance she heard the long lonely whinny of a pony calling across the hills.

TWO
A New Beginning

Slowly Mory became aware of the sunlight on her face. She wanted to stay asleep. She couldn't remember why until she remembered the dream, the wonderful dream of galloping on the black pony. She'd never had such a dream before. She opened her eyes and found Cara looking at her.

"I've brought you some tea," said Cara. "It's by your head." Mory turned her gaze into the sunlight. It hurt her eyes.

"Thanks," she said.

"There's been a change of plan," said Cara. "You and Josh are to stay here while Uncle David and Aunt Sheila get Black Rock ready."

Mory, listening to the lilt of Cara's voice, realised she hadn't heard what she said.

"What?"

"They're saying you're not to go near the place until it's ready. So you can do what you like."

"What on earth is there to do?"

Cara lost patience.

"We're not complete bumpkins, you know. We do have television and radio and washing machines and towns and table tennis in Wales. And, surprising as it may seem, there are lots of things to do here if you stop moaning and look and see." Fancy having to share her room with Mory, who didn't want to be there, who didn't like the farm or Wales or anything very much! Josh was much nicer even if he was younger. Much, much nicer than his miserable sister.

Mory sat up to hide her embarrassment.

"Thanks for the tea," she said, not knowing what else to say.

"You don't need to keep thanking me," said Cara. She got off the bed and drew back the curtains. "It's a really nice day if you can be bothered to notice. I've got to make you breakfast so I hope you're getting up soon." With that she left.

Mory sighed. She'd got off to a really bad start with Cara. All her fault, of course. She stood up and went to the window. What she saw in the sunlight did not match yesterday's memory. Her gaze went to the furthest distance and she saw the land fall away, marked out in squares, oblongs and rectangles by walls and hedges – a glorious patchwork of green. Looking in the other directions, steep hills grew into mountains and beyond the mountains, clear blue sky. It was a breathtaking view and quite unexpected.

"It's beautiful," she said out loud. "I had no idea."

The kitchen was empty when Mory arrived downstairs. She wanted to try out the stove and put the kettle on but didn't like to. The back door opened and a pair of boots flopped to the utility room floor. It was Cara. She held out two eggs.

"For you. One or two?"

"One, please," said Mory.

"Boiled?"

"Yes, fine."

"I'll have the other one then."

It crossed Mory's mind that the eggs had come from a henhouse and were fresh.

"We're lucky today," said Cara. "We've got new hens. They're only just beginning to lay." She seemed to have forgotten her irritation, so Mory asked.

"Can I put the kettle on? How do I do it?"

"It's easy. Just lift the lid. Don't forget to put it down after so you don't lose the heat."

It pleased Mory to lift the lid and boil the kettle as it did watching the eggs boil and buttering the toast. She was hungry and ate a good breakfast.

"Where are the others?" she asked when she had finished.

"Mum's down at Black Rock with Aunt Sheila and Uncle David. Josh and Dad have gone with Mab to check some sheep. When Josh gets back he's going to ride Misty."

Mory remembered her dream and wanted to say, Can I ride Misty too? But she couldn't bring herself to.

"Are there loose ponies round here?" she asked instead.

"You mean wild ones? Not round here. Out on the hills there are."

The image of the black pony drifted before her eyes and faded. Mory nearly said, I saw one, but changed her mind. She might not be believed. She wondered what she was going to do with the day. Its long hours stretched ahead of her.

"Has the furniture lorry arrived?" she asked.

"At the crack of dawn. That's why no one's here. You took ages to wake up. Mum said I had to wait for you."

"Heavens!" said Mory. "I've forgotten Splodge."

"He's fed," said Cara. "I fed him when I fed the others." She loaded the dirty plates into the dishwasher.

"I'm going to see him," said Mory, leaping up. "Thanks."

At the door she muttered her thanks again, feeling uncomfortable, then fled to put on the wellies Cara had lent her the day before.

Mory was feeling almost cheerful as she opened the top stable door. She was met by a mournful mew. Splodge stretched in his basket and blinked. Mory closed the bottom door behind her and picked him up, holding him to her and nuzzling his soft fur with her nose. Slowly Splodge relaxed and began to purr.

"Good puss!" said Mory. "You've got to stay in here for your own good. We don't want you walking back to Waring, do we? If it were up to me I'd have you upstairs. Still, it's nice and cosy here and in a few days you'll be able to go outside."

Mory lay on the straw and Splodge settled comfortably on her chest and enjoyed his nose and eyes being stroked. She lay like that until Josh popped his head over the door.

"Hi, you!" he said. "I'm going to ride Misty. Want to watch?"

"All right," said Mory. She couldn't think of anything better to do. She picked Splodge up and gently put him in his basket, but he jumped straight out and Mory had to squeeze herself through the door to stop him following her.

As she was bolting the top door Cara came into the yard, leading a grey pony on a halter.

"This is Misty," she said.

"Hello, Misty," said Mory.

"Do you think I'm going to like riding?" asked Josh in a jokey sort of way. "I'm bound to fall off." He was nervous.

"You won't," said Cara. She led Misty into the stable next to Splodge.

"Do you want to groom him, Josh?"

"All right."

Josh was brave. Neither he nor Mory had ever had anything to do with ponies before.

"He's really kind," said Cara. "A complete softie. He'll let you do anything with him. This is a dandy brush. Give him a good going over with that."

Misty was looking over the stable door with

curiosity at the two people he hadn't met before, when Josh opened the door and squeezed past him. He turned round and gave Josh a nudge with his nose. Cara laughed.

"He does that. It's his favourite trick!" Josh got over his surprise and tentatively began to brush him. Misty didn't seem to mind at all.

"Go on, really brush him," said Cara. "He likes it!" Josh put his back into it. Misty stood quite still with his eyes half closed.

"Where do you keep his saddle and things?" Mory asked.

"I'll show you."

Mory followed Cara in through a door in the corner of the yard and wondered, for the first time, if Cara had any friends nearby. The farm was isolated. They were fifteen miles from the nearest town and three miles from the village of Llantrist where they were going to go to school. There were no buses.

Well, there was a school bus, so they'd been told, but no other sort of buses.

It was gloomy in the little room where Cara kept her pony things. As Mory's eyes became accustomed to the lack of light she saw an old chest of drawers, a chair, a rickety table and a saddle sitting on a bracket on the wall with a bridle hanging underneath it. Along one wall were pinned several rosettes of different colours.

"Did you win those?" Mory asked.

"Yes. Misty's really good at jumping." said Cara. "Look, in the winter I can light this. It gets nice and warm. It's lovely cleaning tack in here – really cosy." Cara pointed to the corner, where Mory saw an old stove with a metal chimney pipe going up through the roof.

"It's a proper den you've got," said Mory.

"It's my own place."

"It's nice."

Cara looked at Mory, unsure, then picked up the saddle and bridle and went out. Mory stayed behind for a few moments, her face assuming a thoughtful expression. Cara must have to do everything by

herself. It was lucky she had Misty. Mory wondered if having a pony was like having a dog.

She rejoined the others as Josh was putting the final touches to Misty's appearance. All the mud had gone from his coat and his mane was brushed neatly onto one side. Cara was picking his feet out with a hoof pick.

"Do you do this every time?" Josh asked.

"What, feet?"

"No, all of it."

"Well, sometimes I don't do it very well because I'm in a hurry," said Cara.

"That's how I would be, I think," said Josh. "In a hurry."

Cara dropped the hoof pick into her grooming box and put the reins over Misty's neck. She held the bit with one hand and with a fluid movement it was in Misty's mouth and she was popping his ears under the headpiece. She did up the throat lash and nose band and lifted the saddle gently onto his back.

All through this procedure Misty stood quietly, even when his girth was done up. Mory was impressed. She went to the stable door for a closer look. Misty lifted his nose towards her and nuzzled at her hand. His whiskers tickled her palm and she was surprised at his gentleness. She stroked his nose. It was silky soft. She ran her hand down the front of his face.

"He likes being scratched round his ears," said Cara.

Obediently Mory scratched the bottom of an ear and felt Misty lean into her hand.

"He's really nice, isn't he?" said Josh.

"Yes," said Cara. "He is."

Mory followed Josh, Cara and Misty to the field. She stopped at the gate and watched. Cara rode Misty at a walk, then a trot, then a canter. Mory liked the way he carried his tail behind him as he moved.

"Looks easy enough," she thought.

When Josh got on she could see that it wasn't as easy as all that. Josh looked more or less all right at the walk but when Misty trotted he bounced all over the place. Cara was full of encouragement. Josh laughed a lot. He was enjoying himself.

Mory felt out of it and decided to leave them to it. She walked back to the yard, out through the gate and, with a big sigh, took the track which led down to Black Rock Farm, her eyes skimming the steep slope for the black pony but seeing only grass and heather moorland towering into the blue sky.

THREE

Night Visitor

As she rounded the final bend in the track Mory saw the furniture lorry. It seemed huge, bigger than the house. The removal men were sitting on the garden path drinking mugs of tea. The lorry was empty, the unloading finished. Mory walked shyly past the men to the front door.

"Come on, lads!" said one of them. "Back to civilisation." They rose, leaving their mugs on the wall. With great skill the driver backed the lorry into the yard. He waited while the others climbed aboard, gave a toot and waved at Mory. Mory lifted an arm in reply as the lorry set off slowly up the rutted track on its way back to Waring.

Picking up the mugs Mory struggled to open the front door. As she did so, she tried to think of the house as home. With their own things in it perhaps it would be easier. The house didn't smell so strongly today. She squeezed past some tea chests in the hall and bumped into her mother coming out of the kitchen.

"Hello, love," said Sheila, planting a kiss on Mory's head. "I didn't expect you here today. Didn't Cara tell you?"

"I decided to come anyway. I might as well get used to it. The men have just gone."

"I heard the lorry. Pop the mugs in the sink and I'll show you something."

Mory did as she was asked and followed her mother up the wooden staircase to her room. The purple door and the cupboard door had gone. She looked back along the landing. All the doors had gone. Her bedroom floor was piled high with scraps of old wallpaper. The walls were stripped bare except the fireplace wall.

"I did this last night after you'd gone to bed. Didn't have the energy to finish, which is a shame," Sheila said. "Once we've sorted things out a bit we'll get cracking on the decorating. Dad and I are going to camp here while you and Josh stay at Llangabby. It'll be nice for Cara – give you a chance to get to know each other."

"Where are the doors?" asked Mory.

"Dad took them off last night. He and Aunt Olwen have taken them into Aberdawl to get them stripped. They looked a bit precarious on the roof rack. I hope they stayed on. We thought the doors'd be nice just plain wood, but you can paint yours if you like."

"Shall I help unpack?"

"We've been at that all morning. The lorry arrived nice and early. The kitchen's almost sorted."

"Then I'll scrape," said Mory, picking up the scraper she saw on the mantelpiece.

"Fine," said Sheila. "They'll be back soon with supplies, food and decorating stuff. The removal men were wonderful. We're getting on like a house on fire." She disappeared downstairs.

With the sun streaming in the window and most of the wallpaper gone the room didn't seem quite so drab. Mory admired its shape: the fireplace wall with its alcoves, the window wall with the ceiling sloping past it on either side.

She looked out. The house rested comfortably in its dip and the craggy hill opposite seemed close enough to touch. Beyond the hill the land rose. At the top Llangabby Farm stood a sentinel before the panorama she remembered seeing from Cara's bedroom window. There was no breathtaking expanse here but a sense of being cradled. She went into Josh's room which was at the back of the house. Here was the farmyard surrounded by outbuildings and the land opening out into a valley of fields between two hills. Black Rock Farm felt comfortable, Mory decided.

Back in her own room she picked up the scraper and resolved to make the best of Wales. Her room would be nice. There was plenty of space for her bed, table and chair and she could hang all her clothes in the alcove cupboard. Her chest of drawers would fit in the other alcove and there'd be room for the zed bed when Hannah came to stay. Splodge would share her bed of course, and could join her as soon as the room was finished. The sooner the better. When Sheila put her head around the door a few moments later Mory was scraping furiously.

By the end of the day Mory had achieved a wall-paper-free room. As they bounced their way back up to Llangabby in the car, although tired, Mory felt a tremendous sense of achievement. She was positively cheerful at the meal the two families shared. Olwen and Sheila exchanged satisfied glances.

Before she went to bed Mory promised Splodge a new home in a few days. He seemed resigned to his stable and didn't try to follow her out, but she hated having to shut him in. She missed the warm furry bundle on her bed and the contented purr that sent her to sleep.

For the next two days Mory worked hard on her room. She cleaned the windows and washed down the paintwork. Josh and Cara scraped wallpaper in Josh's room. It wasn't long before screams and shouts of merriment brought Sheila upstairs. The pair of them were chucking bits of paper everywhere. Sheila sent them packing. Josh wasn't

really bothered what his room looked like, he was happier out of doors. For Mory her room was an important focus. It meant home and belonging. She felt she really could belong to Black Rock once all her things were neatly arranged and she could see furry, familiar Splodge curled up on her duvet.

David busied himself pasting up thick lining paper on the walls. Next he sanded the floorboards, a noisy, messy business. He ended up looking like a yellow snowman. Mory and Sheila spent ages brushing the sawdust off him.

"Get off! Leave me alone!" he'd shouted as they

chased him round and round the room with the vacuum cleaner. Vacuuming up the dust took ages. David painted a revoltingly smelly sealant on the floor which, once dry, made it a pleasure to walk on. The dark stained boards became golden, streaked with wavy lines of wood grain. Mory put down dust sheets and painted the walls and ceiling white. Sheila painted the skirting boards and window frame. The room looked and smelt fresh.

When David brought home the stripped pine doors he brought some grate blacking as well. Mory was delighted and carefully re-blacked the little fireplace grate. The effect was plain and simple, just what she wanted. Her parents carried up her furniture: the bed, the table, the chair, the chest of drawers. Mory had them move the bed three times and was going to try a fourth position when they rebelled.

"We're not moving it again!" they said, and so it stayed where it was. The chest of drawers fitted the alcove perfectly and her clothes, when she unpacked them, hung behind the pine cupboard door. The room was perfect. Well almost.

"It needs a picture," said Mory and she decided to draw one before she went to bed.

"Now," said her exhausted mother. "Do you think you'll like it here?"

"Yes," said Mory. "Can I fetch Splodge and sleep here tonight?"

"Dad'll run you up to fetch him and your things," said Sheila. "Won't you, David?"

"I will if my old bones can move," he said.

"Let's go!" cried Mory.

"The young have no sympathy for the old," complained her father.

Splodge wasn't pleased to be locked in his basket once again, and mewed pitifully.

"It's all right," Mory told him. "You're going to your new home." Splodge didn't seem to care, and mewed again. Dad put Mory's suitcase in the boot and she climbed in the back with Splodge.

"Can I come?" Cara asked.

"'Course you can," said David. "Hop in the back with Mory."

The car bounced down the track with Splodge wedged between the girls, protesting all the way.

"Poor Splodge," said Cara.

"You're going to have to keep him locked in your room," said Sheila. "I've put the cat tray up there and some water. Rather you than me."

"I don't care about the smelly tray, I'll have Splodge," said Mory. "The tray won't be for long anyway."

"That's love and devotion for you," said Sheila. David laughed.

"It certainly is. The cat tray stinks."

Upstairs in her room Mory put the basket on the floor and undid the straps. Cara shut the door.

"Do you think I'd better close the window?" she said. Mory looked up.

"Yes. thanks," she said. "I'd forgotten it was open. It'd be awful if he got on the roof."

Splodge's head poked from the basket. "Where am I now?" he seemed to be thinking. He jumped out, sniffed and began cautiously to explore, moving slowly, his tummy close to the floor. The girls sat side by side on the bed and watched him.

"I do want him to like his new home," said Mory.

"He will. He'll soon get used to it," said Cara.

"Like me. I'm sorry I was so grotty when we first got here," said Mory. She slid from the bed to the floor. "Well, what do you think of it, Splodge?" Cara laughed.

Splodge was exploring under the bed. He crouched there, surveying the room.

"I hope he sleeps on the bed tonight," said Mory. "Splodge, this is your new home."

There was a knock at the door and Sheila squeezed herself round it, looking for the cat.

"Where is he?"

"Under the bed. He doesn't want to come out," said Mory.

"He will. Give him a chance to settle. It's nearly supper time. We're ready to go up to Llangabby. Olwen said seven-thirty sharp."

The two girls smiled at each other and followed

Sheila from the room, shutting the door behind them.

Mory and her parents returned to Black Rock as dusk was falling. The porch light glowed a cheerful welcome. Mory watched a large moth flutter towards it. A dark shape, the size of a small bird, flitted above the apple tree and was gone.

"What was it?" Mory asked.

"A bat, I think," replied David. "I expect it lives in the barn."

Mory thought back to a lesson at school. Bats: little furry creatures with umbrella wings and feet like hooks to hang upside down with.

Sheila took a deep breath.

"The air smells so . . ." She paused.

"Of the country," Mory finished for her.

"Yes, that's it," laughed Sheila. "Bedtime for you, young lady. It's late."

But before she got into bed Mory took out a large sheet of paper and her special pastels. A picture flashed into her mind. Her fingers worked hard, flying this way and that to capture the image. It was the black pony in the mist. Pleased with her effort, she pinned it to the wall above the bed.

"The finishing touch," she said. "I wonder if I'll see you again."

She switched off the light and stared into the blackness. Now she was sleeping at Black Rock for the first time. It was the start of an adventure, just as her mother had said. Her eyelids grew heavy and she began to drift.

"Night, night, Splodge!" she murmured. In no time she was fast asleep.

She awoke with a start as it was beginning to get light. Something moved on her feet. Slowly Mory sat up. The house was still, her room stuffy. Mory felt down the bed and her hand met the warmth of Splodge's fur. She was delighted to find him there.

A noise drew her attention outside. It sounded like hoofbeats. Mory's first reaction was to think that Misty had got out. The hoofbeats stopped. Skirting the outline of her furniture Mory made her way to the window. She opened it quietly.

A dark shape stood on the track. It moved closer. A pony, now fully visible, stopped outside the front gate and looked up. It wasn't Misty – his grey coat would have shown up lighter. This pony was dark. A strange tingling swept from Mory's head to her heels.

"Hello, pony!" whispered Mory. The pony tensed at the sound of her voice. It was the black pony. Mory knew it.

"So you've come back!" Instinctively Mory put all her gentleness into her voice. The pony let out a low whicker in reply.

"Stay there," whispered Mory. "Please stay

there." She closed the window and pulled on her trainers. Flipping over the velcro fasteners, she crept quickly onto the landing, pulling the door closed behind her. She lowered herself carefully onto each stair. She picked up an apple from the fruit bowl on the kitchen table, along with a piece of baler twine David had left there.

Mory opened the front door. She trembled. Yes, the pony was still there, waiting.

"You knew I wanted you to come back," she said

under her breath, walking slowly to the gate. The pony watched every movement with sharp, pricked ears. Opening the gate Mory held out the apple. The pony put its teeth around it and pulled. Mory held tight to the bottom half and the apple split. The pony ate and Mory, her heart pounding, slipped the twine around its neck. The pony, quite unconcerned, nuzzled her hand for the rest of the apple.

"Have you come to be mine? Have you?" she said gently. The pony pushed at her with its muzzle. Mory pulled on the twine and the pony moved forward. Thrilled at her success, she led the pony into the yard and headed for the paddock at the back of the house.

FOUR

Midnight Dancer

"You've done what?" said David, half waking.

"I've caught a pony and put it in the paddock," said Mory. Sheila didn't stir.

"What time is it?" asked David, turning over.

"A quarter to six."

"Oh, Mory – couldn't this wait until the morning?"

"It is morning."

"Not proper morning."

"But, Dad . . ."

"All right! Make me a cup of tea, will you? I'll get up. Might as well now you've woken me. We'll leave your mum."

Downstairs in the kitchen Mory lifted the lid on the stove and put the kettle on. She filled it with enough water for one mug of tea. She wasn't sure if the hot plate would be hot enough to boil water with the fire damped down so she filled the electric kettle too, just in case. Of course the electric kettle boiled ages before the kettle on the stove was even warm. Mory made the tea.

Elated at her daring, Mory remembered how trustingly the pony had allowed itself to be led through the yard, how it had waited while she'd struggled one-handed to undo the chain on the paddock gate. When she'd let it go it hadn't run off but had stood looking at her as if expecting something.

As the sun rose Mory had seen that the pony was truly black, its mane and tail long and unkempt, its hooves chipped and cracked. Yet it didn't seem in the least wild. Smiling, she'd let the pony nuzzle her hand and her pocket looking for something more to eat.

The pony had a streak of white hair in the base of its mane. It was the only white Mory could see on it. There had been a moment when the breeze had rustled the leaves on the overgrown hedge, causing the pony to start, lift its head and become tense and alert.

"It's all right," Mory had said. She had run her hand gently down the pony's neck, once, then twice. The pony relaxed and she had been so pleased.

"Where do you come from?" she had asked as the pony wandered off a few paces. As if forgetting her it had begun to eat. It was then that Mory wanted to tell someone what she had done and had run to her parents' bedroom.

"Right," said David as he came into the kitchen. "Where's the tea?"

"Sorry to wake you so early," said Mory, handing him a mug.

"Well, I suppose it isn't every day you catch a pony. It came down the track, you say?"

Mory told David exactly what had happened. He could tell his daughter was desperate for him to see this amazing creature. He opened the back door and pulled on his wellies.

"Lead me to it," he said. Carrying his tea he followed Mory across the yard. "Pretty little thing, isn't it?" he said when he saw it. "After breakfast you'd better pop up and ask Glyn to have a look at it. It must belong to someone."

"But it can't," said Mory. "It's got no shoes on and you can see it's not been brushed."

"That doesn't mean it isn't owned," said Dad. "Even the wild ponies belong to someone."

"But I want to keep it."

"I thought ponies weren't your thing. It's Josh that's learning to ride."

"I never said that," said Mory. "I want to keep it. I'll learn to ride. I will."

"Mory, this won't do. It's bound to belong to someone."

The disappointment was acute. From the moment she'd put the baler twine around the pony's neck Mory had felt the pony was hers. She wanted to keep it more badly than anything she'd wanted for ages.

"You'd better make sure it's got something decent to drink," said David. "The trough's full of slime."

By the time Mory had emptied, scrubbed and wiped out the disgusting green slime from the water trough, and had carried bucket after bucket of water from the tap in the yard to fill it, she was determined the pony must be hers. It had trotted over to find out what she was doing and when it had discovered water it had taken a drink.

"I never really knew what ponies were like before," she told the pony as she stroked its neck. "You're wonderful."

After breakfast Josh went with Mory up to Llangabby. He too had been taken with the black pony and Mory had told her story again for Josh and Sheila.

"You mean you caught her with baler twine?" Josh said.

"You must be more careful," said her mother. "A strange pony like that – it could have turned on you."

"But it didn't," said Mory. "And I *was* careful." Sheila wasn't convinced.

"Do you think they'll let you keep her?" Josh asked as they arrived at the top of the track.

"Dad said she must belong to somebody, but we've got to find out who first. That could take ages," said Mory.

They found Cara in the yard.

"Guess what?" said Josh.

"What?"

"You tell her," Josh said.

"I caught a pony."

"And she wants to keep it," said Josh.

"What pony?" said Cara. "The wild ones don't come near us. It must be a stray."

"It hasn't got shoes," said Mory, and she told Cara the story. Cara shrugged.

"I wonder whose it is?"

"It's mine," said Mory. "It came to me."

"I didn't know you liked ponies."

"I like this one," said Mory. "It's special." Cara laughed.

"Let's tell Dad," she said. "He'll know what to do."

They found Uncle Glyn in the barn, changing the oil in his tractor. He wriggled out from underneath it and wiped his oily hands on a rag as he listened.

"Must have come from out of the hills," he said. "I wonder . . ." He paused. "I'll pop down and see it later. It'll be fine in the paddock. Have you given it water?"

"Yes."

"Well, that's all you need to do for now, then," smiled Uncle Glyn. "I'll be down later to take a look."

The three children wandered into the yard.

"It's quite a mystery pony, isn't it?" said Cara. "It's not wild and yet it's probably come from out of the hills. All the hill ponies are uncatchable and yet you caught it."

"What I'd like to do is brush it," said Mory. "It's terribly scruffy. Can you lend me a brush?"

"I've got an old dandy brush you can have," said Cara.

"I'd like to tie it up to brush it," said Mory. "Can I borrow one of those head things?"

"Okay," said Cara. "But you'd better be careful. It may never have been tied up before. Make sure you use some twine in case it pulls back."

"Why?" Mory asked.

"Well, if you tie it to the gate with a loop of twine and then tie the halter rope to the twine, if it pulls back the twine will break. It won't hurt itself that way."

"You'll have to show me."

"Fine," said Cara. "Let's catch Misty. I can show you how to do it all with him."

They went into the tack room to collect Misty's headcollar. Cara said she'd lend Misty's halter to Mory and explained the difference between a head-collar and a halter.

"You see the headcollar does up with a buckle at the side and the halter is made of one long piece of rope which slips over the head and pulls tight around the nose. You're supposed to tie a knot in it so it can't overtighten."

Mory looked at Misty's saddle and bridle with new interest. She was going to watch carefully in order to find out how to do everything. It looked complicated. But then new things always do, she reminded herself. Cara collected a handful of pony nuts from the feed bin.

"You can take some if you want," she told Mory. Mory stuffed several handfuls into the pocket of her jeans. They crossed the yard. There were three sheep in the field with Misty.

"To keep him company," said Cara. "If you keep

the black pony they could live together and not be lonely."

"Do ponies get lonely?' asked Mory, feeling ignorant.

"It says in all the books they do. They're a herd animal. Dad says it depends on the pony. Some mind more than others."

Cara called Misty. He raised his head and stared at her. "I'd love him to have a pony friend. Sheep aren't the same, are they?" Cara called again. At last Misty decided he would come and ambled towards them.

"You can always tell what sort of a mood he's going to be in from the moment you call him," said Cara. "He's in a sleepy mood today, which means he'll do everything at half speed until you get him to wake up."

Misty munched a handful of pony nuts as Cara showed Mory how to put on the halter.

"Don't forget to put the rope end round his neck first so that you've got him if he decides to wander off," said Cara. When the halter was on Mory led Misty from the field and into the yard. He plodded beside her.

"Go on, Misty – get along with you!" said Cara.

Outside Misty's stable was a ring with a loop of blue twine hanging from it. Cara put the end of the halter rope through the loop and tied a knot, the quick-release type. Then she pulled the end of the rope to prove how easily it came undone.

"You do it," Cara said. Mory tried but couldn't manage.

"Can you do this, Josh?" Mory asked.

"Yup," said Josh. Mory tried again and did it.

"You'd better brush Misty so you know how to," said Josh. Mory brushed.

"The important thing with ponies," said Cara, "is to remember to be calm and not to make them jump. They're nervous creatures and need to get to know you."

Mory was pleased with her efforts. Misty looked neat and tidy by the time she'd finished. She longed now to go and do the same to the black pony.

Uncle Glyn called across the yard.

"I'm going down to look at the pony. Do you want to come?"

Cara put Misty in his stable and handed Mory the old dandy brush and halter. They ran to the Landrover.

"Well, what do you think?" David asked as Uncle Glyn ran his hands over the black pony. Mory waited impatiently.

"Nice little mare. She needs the farrier. Her feet are a bit of a mess." Uncle Glyn ran his hand down the pony's off-side front leg and tried to pick her foot up. She jumped away from him.

"Steady now," he said. "Doesn't like that, does she?" He tried again. The pony lifted her foot reluctantly, straining away from Uncle Glyn. Her ears were back and her head up.

"Not been handled much, I shouldn't think. Be interesting to know how old she is. Not very by the look of her. When we get the farrier we can ask him to look at her teeth. Bob's reckoned to be good at ageing horses. I'll make some enquiries when I go to market."

Uncle Glyn went into the house with Dad.

"What do you think of her?" Mory asked, smoothing the pony's neck to calm her down.

"She's lovely," said Cara. Mory took off the halter and the pony backed away and cantered to the end of the paddock. "Bet she's never been ridden."

"I'd like to ride her," said Mory. "She's so beautiful. Will you teach me, Cara? Will you, please?"

Cara laughed. "I couldn't teach you on her. She'd have you on the floor in no time. But I will on Misty."

"I've thought of a name for her," said Mory. "Midnight Dancer, because when she moves she dances and because she came in the middle of the night."

"You'll have to handle her lots so she trusts you," said Cara. "She's not wild but then she's not quite tame either."

"Yes," said Mory. "I want her to trust me more than anything. I'll never let her down." From the other end of the field the pony whinnied. "She's mine. She's meant to be mine. She came to me," said Mory and shivered with excitement.

FIVE

Enquiries

For the next two days Mory spent as much time as she could with Midnight Dancer. She led the pony on the halter, encouraging her all the while, until she became used to it. Mory stroked her and talked to her. At first Dancer was tense and Mory wondered if she was nervous about having her feet picked up. Mory knew that when she did pick them up the pony must understand she wouldn't be hurt. The farrier was coming to shoe Misty next week. Time enough to get Dancer used to having her feet handled.

These days Mory's pockets were full of titbits – bits of apple, carrot or pony nuts. Sheila had complained. There were never any carrots or apples when she wanted them. One morning David was loading the washing machine when a pocketful of pony nuts scattered all over the floor. He was cross even though Mory swept them up.

"It's in a good cause," Mory told him.

Hoping she had judged it right, Mory began the

tying-up training. She fixed a loop of twine to the gate and led Dancer to it. She put the end of the rope through the loop. She didn't tie a knot, but held the end of the rope taut against the loop. When Dancer pulled against the rope she was startled at being held so firmly. Mory quickly released the pressure on the rope and told Dancer how good she was, giving her a piece of carrot at the same time. Mory was determined not to frighten her, however long it took.

Dancer was quick to learn. Mory was soon able to keep the pressure on the rope. Dancer didn't pull against it, but accepted it as the limit of her movement and enjoyed the titbit she received as a reward.

"You're a wonderful girl," Mory told her, offering half an apple. "A good pony." Dancer picked the apple gently off Mory's hand and crunched it appreciatively. For the first time Mory tied a quick release-knot and walked away. Dancer turned and watched her. When she felt the limit of the rope, she moved round in order to see where Mory was going but without any fuss. Mory was delighted.

"Now you've got to learn to be brushed," she told Dancer.

Mory ran her hands all over the pony, right down to her feet, then patted them. Dancer seemed quite happy with that. Mory brushed her with gentle strokes. The pony put her ears back at the swishing noise, but settled and seemed to enjoy it.

"You're a good girl," said Mory. "A good girl."

Dancer's tail was thick and matted with bits of twig and bracken woven into it. Mory began to pick her way through it and pull it apart.

"This is going to take forever," she sighed. Dancer didn't mind. She was enjoying the attention.

"You're doing really well with her," Cara said when she came to see how they were getting on. "She's looking so much better now you've groomed her." Mory gave a demonstration. Dancer walked and trotted by Mory's side.

"Well done," said Cara. "Have you tried picking her feet up yet?"

"Not yet, but I will."

"I think it's time you started riding Misty," said Cara. "You've got lots to learn." Mory agreed. She let Dancer go and the two girls walked up to Llangabby.

Mory's first riding lesson was a rude awakening. Putting Misty's saddle and bridle on was far less difficult than she imagined – it was the rest that was the problem. Wearing Cara's hat and her own green wellies she stood ready. Cara told her how to mount. Springing up, she sat gently in the saddle. That bit was easy. Cara led Misty forward. The strangeness of the movement took Mory by surprise and she nearly lost her balance. Misty was eager to get on. He enjoyed being ridden and Mory wondered how she would stop if Cara let go.

Mory was given masses of instructions. She was to keep her back straight, her heels down and her knees in and on no account to hold herself on to Misty's back with the reins. She was to hold his mane or the saddle and she must keep a light contact with his mouth. What did that mean? Confused, Mory wobbled along doing her best. When Misty trotted she hung on, feeling that at any second she would be bounced to the ground.

"Stop, Cara!" she cried.

Cara and Misty stopped but Mory carried on. She ended up draped over Misty's neck. She heaved herself upright. "I can't do it!" she cried.

"You will," said Cara. "Everyone feels like that when they start. You saw what Josh was like. Have a look at him now. Josh!"

Josh had been watching at the gate. He came over, wearing an annoying know-it-all grin. Mory was furious that he had such a start on her and furious with herself. If only she hadn't been so stand-offish she might have been riding properly by now.

Josh took Misty to a corner of the field. He trotted in a circle, looking positive and confident. Mory had to admit he could do a nice rising trot.

"See?" said Cara. "It doesn't take long."

"Well, if Josh can do it I can," said Mory, steeling herself for another go.

"The secret is to be as relaxed as possible and go with the movement," said Cara.

Mory was hardly relaxed. She wanted to ride so badly, the wanting was making her more and more tense.

"It'll take practice," she told herself. "The important thing is to enjoy it." Enjoying it was difficult as she struggled to find the rhythm of Misty's trot.

By the end of her first lesson, Mory was feeling both elated and desperate. She was less like a sack of potatoes but expected it would take ages for her to be good enough to ride Dancer. She patted Misty and gave him a carrot.

"Thanks for putting up with me, Misty," she said.

"You weren't as bad as you imagine," said Cara. "You sit nicely and you were very aware of his mouth. You never once pulled on the reins. When you felt wobbly you held his mane. It's practice. You need to do it every day."

"But it's only two more weeks till school starts," cried Mory.

"If you ride every day you'll be amazed at how you improve. Besides, the evenings are getting lighter. We can ride after school."

Mory saw all this was true. In spite of its frustrations, her first riding lesson had been a success. Forgotten were her complaints about leaving Waring in the middle of the school year. Her plans ran ahead to the summer holidays, when she would ride Dancer across the hills.

"You'll be able to do shows by then," said Cara. Mory wasn't so sure about that. She didn't really know what you did at shows, although she thought it might be nice to win a rosette.

"I'll ride every day," she said. "I'll get better and better. Soon I shall ride Dancer."

The next day was market day in Aberdawl. Uncle Glyn was going in for some supplies and to make "enquiries" about Midnight Dancer. Aunt Olwen said she'd do her supermarket shop and take the children with her.

Mory was up at the crack of dawn. The first

thing she was going to do was ride. She fed Splodge and let him outside for the first time. He sniffed cautiously before setting out across the yard.

"I hope he comes back," said Mory.

"Of course he will," said Josh. "You've kept him locked up long enough. He's bound to want to explore."

Mory said hello to Dancer and gave her some pony nuts.

"You don't mind being on your own, do you, girl?" she said as the pony nuzzled her hand with her soft nose. Mory patted her gently.

"I've got to go," she told Dancer. "I'm learning to ride. You wait – I'll be riding you soon."

Mory ran up the track to Llangabby. There was no sign of Cara so she fetched Misty's headcollar and went to the field to fetch him. By the time Cara joined her Misty had been groomed and tacked up.

"Can you see if I've done it right?" Mory asked. Cara inspected Misty carefully.

"Perfectly all right," she said.

They led Misty into the field and Mory mounted. She felt a stiffness in her muscles and her seat bones were sore.

"Ouch!" she said. "Is that normal?'

"It is till your muscles get used to it," said Cara.

This time Mory was ready for the movement and was much more balanced. She soon forgot her stiff muscles and began to enjoy herself. Cara let her walk Misty by herself. He very kindly didn't take advantage of her inexperience and went where he was asked.

"I'm getting it!" cried Mory, feeling a tremendous sense of achievement. She watched Cara pop Misty over two jumps at the far end of the field. Misty enjoyed jumping. His ears pricked forward and he flew over them effortlessly.

"One day I'll be able to do that," Mory told herself. Then, turning her mind to the most important matter of the day, she began to wonder what Uncle Glyn would find out at Aberdawl market. Who, if anyone, had lost Midnight Dancer? A chill crept up Mory's spine. It was fear. No one must claim her. No one. She wished as hard as possible and hoped the wish would come true.

Aberdawl was a sleepy little town, or so it seemed to Mory after the bustling crowds of Waring. Everyone seemed to know one another here. She and Josh as the strangers were being stared at. It made her uncomfortable. They left Uncle Glyn in the market to do his chores, and Aunt Olwen drove them to the big supermarket on the edge of town. Mory pushed the trolley while the others went from shelf to shelf filling it. All the while Mory wondered if Uncle Glyn had found anyone who had lost a black pony.

At the checkout Mory nearly dropped a bag of groceries. As it was, two tins of tomatoes rolled across the floor under the feet of an elderly lady. Mory apologised and felt stupid. Cara picked up the tins and helped Mory with the bag.

"Don't worry," she said.

While loading the car the anxiety became unbearable. As Aunt Olwen drove off Mory's dread increased. It was worse than going to the dentist. Aunt Olwen parked the car and as they tumbled out she gave Mory a squeeze.

"We're meeting Glyn in the Market Café. Over

there," she pointed. Mory saw the sign above a shop front. Her face was full of worry as she opened the café door. She saw Uncle Glyn sitting in the corner with another man.

"Who's he?" Mory asked.

"Owen Lewis," said Cara.

Uncle Glyn waved and beckoned them over.

"This is Mr Lewis," he told Mory.

"Hello, Owen," said Olwen, joining them. "I'll get the children a snack." Mory settled for lemonade. She didn't want anything to eat.

"Sit down," said Uncle Glyn. They brought up more chairs and squeezed around the table, which was really too small for all of them.

"Mr Lewis is the owner of your pony," said Uncle Glyn. Something in the way he said it told Mory that Uncle Glyn didn't like this Mr Lewis very much. "The pony belonged to Mr Lewis's father, who made a bit of a pet of it. Old Mr Lewis lived way out in the hills but I'm sorry to say he died a week or two back."

Mory's heart sank. It explained why Dancer was so friendly.

"Now Mr Lewis here wants to put the pony in the pony sales. That's right, isn't it, Mr Lewis?"

Mr Lewis grunted.

"But Mr Lewis also says that we can have the pony if we pay a thousand pounds for it. I've pointed out to Mr Lewis that, in my opinion, the pony isn't worth a thousand pounds but he won't lower the price."

Mory felt herself go cold. Where was she going to get a thousand pounds from? If she had it she'd pay it without question, but she hadn't even got twenty pounds.

"Mr Lewis lives in Aberdawl. He can't keep the pony himself so we're going to keep her for the moment. If he can find someone to buy her for a thousand pounds he will, otherwise she'll go to the pony sales here next week and be sold at auction."

Aunt Olwen was bringing the drinks over as Mory got up and stumbled out of the café. She ran to the cattle pens and leaned unseeing against a pen full of cows. This was where they would sell her pony. It was worse than her worst imaginings. If only she had some money! Mory fought back her tears. Never in her whole life had she felt so desperate. Someone took hold of her hand and held it tight. It was Cara. The tears fell.

SIX

Which Way To Turn

Mory arrived home from the market with red eyes, feeling utterly miserable. Nothing anyone could say would comfort her.

"If only I had some money," she repeated over and over again through her sobs.

Aunt Olwen drove straight to Black Rock. Sheila came out to meet them and opened her arms to her sobbing daughter.

"You must have found the owner," said Sheila. The two families went into the kitchen and Uncle Glyn explained the situation to Sheila and David.

"Old Mr Lewis was a strange old fella. A bit of a hermit if you like. No harm in him, just kept to himself. When I heard the pony had arrived I did wonder. I knew old Mr Lewis had died and had a pony up there with him for a pet. I'm surprised she didn't join the wild ponies, but maybe she came across Black Rock first."

"So who does the pony belong to now?" David asked.

"Owen Lewis, old Mr Lewis's son. He had the cheek to want a thousand pounds for the mare. I ask you! As if I don't know what she's worth," said Uncle Glyn.

"How much is she worth?" Sheila asked.

"She must be about four and unbroken. A nice little Welsh mare, say three hundred and fifty to four hundred, five at the most. But to ask a thousand is daylight robbery. She'll have to prove herself for that sort of money. There's a lot of work to be done on her before anyone can know what she's like as a riding pony."

"He's going to put Dancer in the auction," sobbed Mory. "Anyone could buy her."

"Cara, Josh – take Mory outside for a bit. Go and check on the pony. I want to have a chat, just grown-ups," said Uncle Glyn.

The three young people filed out. They wandered across the yard and leaned over the paddock gate where Dancer was grazing contentedly in the sunshine. There was a miaow and Splodge rubbed himself around Mory's legs. She picked him up.

"I told you he wouldn't go off," said Josh.

Mory buried her face in Splodge's fur and made it wet with tears. Dancer came over to see what was going on and if there were any titbits. She nudged Mory's shoulder with her nose as if to say, Come on, cheer up and give me some pony nuts! Splodge, alarmed at such close proximity to an animal he wasn't familiar with, struggled to get away. Mory let him go and put her arms around Dancer's neck.

"She's so lovely," said Mory. "I can't bear it."

"I don't think you should get so upset," said Josh.

"It's all right for you," said Mory. "You don't feel the same way about her."

"I know how you feel," said Josh. "I do. But I bet there's a way round it."

"I could run away with her," said Mory. "There must be somewhere in the hills we could hide."

"That would only delay things," said Cara. "you'd have to come home in the end. If she misses the pony sales in Aberdawl there are other sales she could go in."

"Well, I've got to do something," said Mory. "If only I could ride her we could go off together easily."

"You're daft," said Cara. "You've got nowhere to go. I think you should try and buy her."

"For a thousand pounds? You must be joking!"

"Well, I can't think what else you can do," said Cara.

Sheila called to them from the back door.

"Come in," she said. "I think we've got a plan."

The three of them ran. Dancer stepped back from the gate in surprise and watched them go. Then she turned, kicked up her heels in a big buck

and trotted in a circle, returning to watch the children go indoors.

"A plan?" cried Mory, bursting into the kitchen. "Will it work? What is it?"

"Calm down," said Sheila, "and listen. It may work and it may not but it's the best we can think of at the moment."

"You tell her, Glyn," said David. Mory's eyes were on fire.

"Now don't get too excited," said Uncle Glyn. "There's an element of risk and you may not end up with Dancer. We'll have to see."

"But what's the plan?" said Mory. "Please, tell me."

"It's to put Dancer in the auction . . ."

"No!" cried Mory. "No!"

"Mory, listen. It's no good if you don't hear Uncle Glyn out. Now calm yourself and listen." Sheila was firm.

"I don't want her to go in the auction," said Mory. "She's mine."

"Be quiet and listen," said Sheila. "We know how you feel about the pony and we're trying to help." Mory subsided onto her chair and chewed her lip.

"Now give me a chance to explain," said Uncle Glyn. "We can't pay a thousand pounds for the pony. It's too much money. But we can bid for her in the auction. We've set a ceiling price of five hundred pounds."

"We simply can't afford any more than that," said David. "There's the pottery to kit out, which involves lots of building. It's going to cost a great deal of money before we get any return on it. To earn five hundred pounds I've got to make a lot of pots."

"I'll help you, Dad, I will," said Mory.

"You do want Dancer instead of a table-tennis table, I suppose?" said Sheila.

"Mummy, I do!" cried Mory, flinging her arms around her mother's neck. "Daddy, thank you!" Mory gave David a bear hug and a kiss. "Thank you."

"I was thinking I might want a pony too," said Josh.

"Don't worry, Josh, we're working on it," said David. "But I don't think your pony is quite as urgent as Mory's, do you?"

"Not quite as urgent," he said guardedly.

"I should point out," said Uncle Glyn, "that the bidding will be in guineas."

"Good heavens!" said David. "Really?"

"What are guineas?" asked Mory.

"Old-fashioned money," said Uncle Glyn. "A guinea is worth one pound and five pence. In old money it used to be twenty-one shillings. For some reason, keeping a tradition I suppose, horses and ponies are still bought and sold in guineas at auction as they always were."

"A quick sum," said David, scribbling on the back of an old envelope. "That means we can spend four hundred and eighty guineas. I'll go the extra four pounds. Four hundred and eighty guineas equals five hundred and four pounds. That's the absolute limit. Do you understand, Mory?"

"But what happens if someone bids more than four hundred and eighty guineas for her?" said Mory.

"That's the chance we have to take," said Uncle Glyn. "But I think we should get her for a lot less than that. I thought of offering five hundred pounds for her now but Owen Lewis is greedy and he's a gambler. If we pay him over the odds he'll take it, but around the odds and he'll wait. So that's what we must do."

"You could try offering him the five hundred pounds," said Sheila.

"Why not?" said Uncle Glyn. "I'll try."

"At least we don't have to wait long," said Aunt Olwen. "Just a week to go to the sales."

"A whole week!" sighed Mory. It seemed like forever and she wondered how she would live through it.

"You've got lots to do," said Sheila. "Have you trained Dancer to pick up her feet yet?"

"Yes," said Aunt Olwen. "Bob the farrier is coming on Tuesday, so you'd better get busy. And I've asked Megan and Ian Reece to come and take a look at the pony."

Cara's face lit up.

"Will they have time to give me a riding lesson?" she asked.

Aunt Olwen smiled. "We'll see," she said.

"Who are the Reeces?" Mory asked.

"Very nice people who run a riding school. They taught Cara to ride on their ponies before she had Misty," said Aunt Olwen.

"It was Megan who found Misty for me," said Cara. "She couldn't have found me a better pony in a million years."

Mory had a lot to think about. She was working from ignorance with Dancer. She had to ask questions and pick Cara's brains all the time. When, for instance, did Cara think she should try and pick up Dancer's feet?

"Whenever it feels right," said Cara. So Mory decided to try it straight away. "I'll help you," said Cara.

With the panic of the morning over Mory began to relax. Cara came with her to catch Dancer, who was happy to come in. Mory's pockets were bulging with rewards. Cara held the halter rope and gently stroked the pony's neck. Mory ran her hands over the pony as she had done so many times before, then went down each leg and tapped Dancer's hooves. Dancer stood quietly. Mory ran her hand down Dancer's near-side front leg again, but instead of tapping her hoof she held the pony's fetlock firmly.

"Pick it up, girl!" she said, nudging Dancer's shoulder, and to her surprise the pony lifted her leg. Mory lowered the foot to the ground and patted the pony. Cara gave her some pony nuts.

"Try the other front leg," said Cara.

Mory went round to the other side and repeated the process. Up came the other leg just as easily.

"Do you want to try the hind legs?" Cara said.

"Might as well," said Mory. Mory ran her hand along Dancer's back and down her inside off hind leg. She grasped the fetlock and tugged. Dancer lifted her leg and then tried to put it down again.

"Hang on," said Cara. "Steady, girl. Steady now." Mory hung on and Dancer settled.

"Well done, Dancer! Well done!" said Mory, patting her and giving her some apple.

"She wasn't sure about that," said Cara. "Why not try the other one?" Mory went round to the other side and ran her hand down Dancer's back. Dancer moved away from her suspiciously.

"It's all right," said Mory. "I just want to lift your leg. I won't hurt you. Come on girl." She ran her hand down Dancer's back again and down her leg. Reluctantly Dancer lifted the foot but she didn't struggle. Mory put it down gently and told her how wonderful she was.

"Might as well go round again," said Cara. "Just so she knows it's all right. She's being very good. She didn't try to kick or anything." Mory was shocked. It hadn't crossed her mind that Dancer might kick.

Mory picked up each foot in turn. Dancer looked at her as if to say, all right, I know what to do now. You can pick them up whenever you like.

"She's got a good temperament." said Cara. "Now she knows what's expected she doesn't mind at all. Next time you do her feet you ought to get a hammer and tap the soles to get her used to what the farrier will do."

"Good idea," said Mory. "I'll do it with her tied up next time. I think she'll be all right." Then she frowned. "How's she going to get to the pony sales? Will I have to walk her there?"

"She'll go in the pony trailer," said Cara.

"Will she go in just like that?"

"If she won't, Dad'll make her. She's got to go to the market."

Mory didn't want Dancer forced to do anything.

"Misty goes in all right," said Cara. "I'm sure Dancer will. I tell you what – I'll ask Dad if we can turn the ponies out together. When they're used to each other we can put Misty in the trailer and try Dancer. If another pony's already in it she'll probably go in easily."

"It's worth a try, isn't it?" said Mory.

Uncle Glyn was happy enough for them to do that and suggested they take Misty down to Black Rock. It was Mory who wanted to take Dancer up to Llangabby.

"I've never walked her anywhere but in the paddock," she said. "I want to see what she's like."

"If you want," said Uncle Glyn. "But I shall come with you just in case."

"I'm sure she'll be fine," said Mory. "She learns really fast."

Nevertheless Uncle Glyn insisted and met them at the paddock as Mory was fetching Dancer.

"She's got guts," he remarked to his daughter.

"She's good with Dancer," said Cara. "They like one another."

Mory led Dancer to the gate. Dancer was expecting to be tied to it as usual so when it opened she looked a little surprised. She walked into the yard with ears pricked and minced sideways as Splodge made a mad dash in front of her.

"Don't hold her quite so tightly," said Uncle Glyn. "Give a little pull and let go if she's not going quite the way you want her to."

With this advice Mory led the way up the track to Llangabby. Dancer looked this way and that, but she didn't misbehave and soon settled to a steady walk. Mory was proud of her. Before they turned into the yard Uncle Glyn spoke.

"Be careful when she sees Misty," he said.

"Don't let her pull you over."

It was well that Mory was forewarned, for when Misty let out a whinny of greeting Dancer surged forward. Mory held her firmly and the pony stayed in check.

"I think we should turn them out and let them get on with it, don't you?" said Uncle Glyn.

"Might as well," said Cara.

Misty was snorting with excitement. Uncle Glyn opened the gate and pushed him back.

"Bring Dancer in," he told Mory. "But before you take the halter off, turn her to face the gate. Back, Misty!"

Mory did as she was told. She was glad she had, for when she let Dancer go she swung round with a mighty buck to face Misty. By that time Mory was well out of the way. The two ponies sniffed noses until Dancer squealed and stamped her foot. Misty pranced around her. Bucking and kicking for all she was worth Dancer set off down the field. Misty followed in pursuit. They tore up and down like mad things. Mory was amazed.

"What makes you think they're pleased to see each other?" she laughed.

"They'll soon settle," said Uncle Glyn, and calling Mab, he set off to see to his sheep.

SEVEN

Preparations

The following day Mory was there when a beaten-up blue car turned into the yard at Llangabby and Owen Lewis got out. Luckily Uncle Glyn was in the barn, for Mory was scared that Mr Lewis might take Dancer away. "I've come to check up on my mare," he said.

"She's over here, Owen. Out with my daughter's pony," said Uncle Glyn, leading the way. The ponies were grazing contentedly side by side. "She's being well looked after, as you can see."

Owen Lewis nodded.

"Had any thoughts on the price?" he asked after a pause.

"We'll make you an offer of five hundred pounds," said Uncle Glyn.

"Pah!" said Mr Lewis. "Eight hundred is my final offer and worth every penny."

"No thanks, Owen. Five hundred is an exceptionally good price for her and you know it."

"I'll be up at eight on Wednesday to collect

her," said Mr Lewis, irritated.

"We'll be bidding for her at the sales," said Uncle Glyn. "I'll be happy to take her in." Mr Lewis's eyes narrowed. He looked at Uncle Glyn and gave a curt nod.

"I'll see you there," he said and walked to his car. He reversed out of the yard with not even a wave.

"A slippery character," said Uncle Glyn to Mory. He put his arm around her shoulder. "Don't worry. My old bones tell me all will be well."

Cara was sorry she'd missed Owen Lewis's visit. She wished she'd seen his face when her father had refused to pay eight hundred pounds for Dancer.

"It's all very well," said Mory. "But what happens if someone is willing to pay eight hundred pounds for her?"

"They won't be. I don't suppose anyone local will bid for her when they know what Owen Lewis has been up to."

"They might if they want her enough," said Mory. "She's so lovely."

"She may not be so lovely to ride and even you don't know that yet," said Cara. Josh joined them.

"Can I have the first lesson?" he asked. "I want to go with Uncle Glyn to check the sheep."

Cara fetched Misty. He didn't want to leave Dancer, who whinnied after him as he was led away.

"They'll have to get used to being separated," said Cara.

When Misty was tacked up it was time for Dancer to be put in the stable.

"What do you think she'll make of that?" asked Mory.

"You're going to find out," said Cara. Mory put the halter on Dancer and led her through the yard and into Misty's stable. Josh closed the door behind her. She seemed a little surprised to find herself there, sniffed the floor a bit and looked out over the door. Mory offered her a piece of carrot which she accepted, crunching it with relish.

"Leave her to get used to it. She will," said Cara.

Mory leaned over the field gate, half watching Josh ride but with her mind on the auction. When it was her turn she rode better than before, perhaps because she wasn't trying so hard, her mind being preoccupied with the pony sales. Cara was really pleased with her pupils.

Aunt Olwen told them Megan and Ian Reece were coming on Friday afternoon and they'd offered to help load Dancer in the trailer for the first time.

"I know," said Mory, stroking Dancer's nose. "So much has happened to you since you arrived. Completely new things. But you're very good about them. Now you're not to mind about the trailer."

Friday afternoon came and Mory was nervous. How would Dancer feel, a pony who had always been in open spaces, confined in such a small space with nowhere to turn? Cara reassured her.

"She won't mind at all. Your problem is that you've always got to have something to worry about."

Mory stuck out her tongue.

"That's more like it! At least when you're rude you're not worrying!"

When a green Landrover turned into the yard Cara, Mory and Josh were waiting. The trailer was hitched up ready. Mory liked Megan and Ian Reece at once. There was something open and friendly about them both.

"Well," said Megan, "you must be Mory and you Josh." She shook hands with them both. "Welcome to Wales."

"How are you liking it so far?" Ian asked as he too shook them warmly by the hand.

"It's great," said Mory shyly.

Aunt Olwen joined them. Megan and Ian chatted away, filling Aunt Olwen in on the local gossip.

"You get out of touch here," said Olwen. "There's always so much to do that I haven't been to the W.I. for ages."

"What's that?" Mory asked.

"The Women's Institute," said Cara, pulling a face.

"Well, show us this new pony. We can't wait," said Megan. "We've already heard so much about it from Cara."

Mory, halter in hand, led the way to the field. She hoped that Dancer would show herself off to full advantage. Both ponies were waiting by the gate. The strange voices must have aroused their curiosity. Mory gave Dancer some pony nuts and slipped the halter over her head. Cara put on Misty's headcollar. The girls led the ponies into the yard.

Megan and Ian ran experienced eyes over Dancer.

Mory walked her up and down for them.

"Trot her for us, will you, Mory?" Megan asked. Mory trotted Dancer up and down. She was as good as gold.

"She's nice," said Ian. "Lovely movement."

"Before you say anything about her feet," said Aunt Olwen, "the farrier's coming on Tuesday."

"She's a lovely pony," said Megan. Mory glowed with pride.

Uncle Glyn joined them and it was down to the serious business of asking Dancer to go in the trailer. It was parked alongside the barn wall with the front and back ramps down. Cara led Misty up the back ramp and he walked inside happily.

"Come on, Dancer. You saw what Misty did. It's easy," said Mory as she led Dancer towards the ramp. Dancer didn't think so. She put one foot on the ramp and went backwards.

"Don't pull," said Megan. Ian went to the Land-rover and fetched a lungeing rein. "It's a lot to ask," Megan went on. "We'll take our time." Ian fixed the lungeing rein to the side of the trailer. It was a long, flat, white rope.

Something else I'll have to ask about, thought Mory, who had no idea what a lungeing rein was for, although she could see it might be useful now.

"Lead her up again," said Megan, and Mory did so. She felt Dancer hesitate. Ian came quietly round behind her with the lungeing rein, which touched

her above the hocks. At that moment, as if on cue, Misty gave a little whicker from inside the trailer. He seemed to be saying, Come on in. It's fine in here.

Dancer took two hesitant steps up the ramp and Ian gently pressed the lungeing rein against her. Misty whickered again and Dancer walked up the ramp and in. Megan lifted the ramp before Dancer could think of backing out and Mory gave her lots of pony nuts and praise.

"Bring her out and do it again," said Megan. Mory led Dancer out of the front of the trailer. Megan put down the back ramp. Dancer walked into the trailer as if she'd been doing it all her life.

"What a good pony," said Megan. "Practice every day and you shouldn't have any trouble on Wednesday, going or coming back."

"*If* we bring her back," thought Mory.

"We'll be there anyway, if you need help," said Ian.

"Right," said Aunt Olwen. "Now we can all go in for tea."

Mory and Cara turned the ponies out and joined the others in the kitchen. Aunt Olwen had baked scones, which made the kitchen smell inviting. Cara and Josh tucked in and covered their scones with lashings of jam. Mory managed to eat one. She'd stopped feeling hungry.

"You've done well with Dancer," said Megan. "You should be pleased. Especially as you haven't had anything to do with ponies before." Mory blushed.

"I want to do it all by myself if she stays mine," she said.

"I'm sure you will," said Megan. "But remember that Ian and I are always happy to help. Have you got a saddle and bridle?"

"No," stumbled Mory. She hadn't thought that far ahead. "I was hoping Cara would lend me hers."

"Well, that won't be any good when you want to go out riding together," laughed Ian. "Who's going to go bareback?"

"Will it be very expensive?" Mory asked.

"Don't worry, I'm sure we'll be able to fix you up with something," said Megan. "We'll lend you a lungeing rein if you like."

"I've got one," said Cara.

"Well, there you are then."

"What's a lungeing rein for?" asked Mory, wishing she wasn't so ignorant.

"It's so the pony can walk, trot and canter round you in circles. They learn commands and to be obedient and it supples them up. You do it before you sit on them for the first time, so that when you do ride them they've had some training," Megan explained. "I think you're in need of a book. I'll lend you the one I lent to Cara – it's very good. And you can come and watch us at work if you like."

"Thank you," said Mory.

"After the auction you'll be able to get cracking," said Ian.

Everyone seemed to think that Dancer would be Mory's, except Mory herself. She was terrified that someone would outbid them. She tried to stay calm but her anxiety showed more and more by the dark shadows that came around her eyes. By Tuesday she could no longer eat anything for worrying. It was the day of the farrier. Bob arrived in his van to shoe Misty and trim Dancer's feet.

"Let her watch me do Misty," said Bob. He was

a tall, wiry man. Mory liked him. He had strong hands which were slow to move. When he pushed Misty into place they were gentle on the pony's rump. Dancer watched at first but soon stopped bothering. She was alarmed only when Bob pressed the hot shoe onto Misty's foot and clouds of pungent hoof smoke filled the air. She didn't mind the banging of the hammer on the shoe as Bob hit it into shape on the anvil. She stayed calm.

"Misty's a good influence," said Cara.

"Indeed he is," said Bob, as he knocked a nail into the shoe and broke off the end where it had come through the wall of the hoof. "He's a good little pony. A little cracker. If he's not alarmed she knows she needn't be. It's a good way for them to learn."

Then it was Dancer's turn. Bob stood for a moment and rubbed her head.

"Hello, old girl," he said. Then he turned and slowly ran his hand down her off-side front leg, picked it up, pulled it between his legs and with his big clippers snipped around the horn, which fell in a piece to the ground. Dancer stood without a murmur. Bob rasped the rough edges smooth and cut back the frog with a knife. He did the same for each foot.

"That looks a bit better," he said.

By the time Uncle Glyn came over Bob had finished. Mory gave Dancer a whole carrot and a lot of pats.

"It'll take time for her hoofs to come right," said Bob, "but they could have been worse." He put his equipment back in the van.

"Can you tell us how old she is?" Mory asked.

"Always a tricky one, that," said Bob. "I'll have a go but don't hold me to it."

Bob took hold of Dancer's jaws and opened her mouth. Dancer didn't like this, but he was firm and had a good look at her front teeth.

"And the considered opinion is?" asked Uncle Glyn.

"I'd say four," said Bob. "Rising five."

"Quite a youngster," said Uncle Glyn.

"Good luck at the sales!" Bob said to Mory. "I hope you get her. She's nice."

That night Mory found it difficult to sleep. Splodge lay on the bottom of her bed as she tossed and turned at the top. She woke early with her stomach tied in a tight knot. Struggling out of bed, she staggered to the bathroom where Sheila found her, wondering if she was going to be sick.

EIGHT

The Pony Sales

Mory's anxiety was infectious and everyone seemed on edge when they got up. It was an early start. On no account could Mory be persuaded to eat anything, but she managed to drink a glass of water. Sheila worried over her, imagining her daughter fading away before her eyes.

"She'll eat when it's all over," said David.

"If she gets the pony," said Sheila. "If she doesn't . . . well, I just don't know what she'll be like."

Mory sat upstairs in her bedroom absent-mindedly stroking Splodge. Suddenly she jumped up and ran to the bookshelves Sheila had made for her. On the bottom shelf was her money hedgehog. She shook it, then flung it on the bed and ran to Josh's room. Josh, searching for a shoe under the bed, looked up in surprise.

"How much money have you got?" Mory asked.

"I don't know. More than ten pounds."

"Can I borrow it?"

"What for?"

"How can you say that? For Dancer! In case the bidding goes over four hundred and eighty guineas," said Mory. "I'll pay it back, I promise I will." Josh considered the request.

"Okay," he said, reaching for the tin he kept his money in. "Let's have a look." He emptied the money on the bed and started counting. Mory rushed back to her hedgehog and pulled out the stopper. She counted six pounds fifty-three pence and cursed herself for not saving her pocket money like Josh did. She met him on the landing, where he handed her his savings.

"Eleven pounds fifty," he said.

"Thanks a million, Josh!" said Mory. She stuffed the money in her pocket and headed for the stairs.

"Where're you going?"

"Llangabby. To see how much money Cara's got and to get Dancer ready, of course."

"I'll come with you."

"We're going on up," Mory told her parents, who were still drinking tea in the kitchen.

"We'll follow in a few minutes," said David.

"I'll be glad when this auction is over," said Sheila as the back door slammed. "Life isn't going to be worth living if she doesn't get this pony. Couldn't we run to a bit more?"

"You know we can't, love. If we do it jeopardises everything. And what about Josh? He wants a pony as well now."

"You're right, we can't." Sheila let out a big sigh and stared glumly at her mug.

Mory and Josh raced into the yard at Llangabby, pulled off their boots, and went into the kitchen. Everyone was sitting round the kitchen table finishing breakfast.

"You're nice and early," said Aunt Olwen. "It's not eight o'clock yet."

"I've brought the ponies in," said Cara.

"I'm not grooming Dancer," said Mory. "I want her to look as scruffy and horrible as possible so no one will want her but me."

"I've given Misty a going over," said Cara as she got up from the table.

When they got to the utility room Mory pounced.

"Cara, lend me all your money," she said.

"What for?" asked Cara.

"In case I need it for the auction. So far I've got eighteen pounds and three pence."

"Oh, Mory!" said Cara. "I've just bought Misty a new numnah. I've hardly got anything. But you can have what's left."

Cara went back indoors. Mory put her thumb in her mouth and did something she hadn't done for ages – chew her nail. Before she'd even realised it she'd ripped a piece off. She spat the nail on the floor and watched the blood ooze from the torn skin.

"Mory!" said Josh. "You spat!"

"I didn't."

"And you've made your thumb bleed. I thought you didn't bite your nails any more."

"Shut up!" said Mory, storming into the yard. She could hardly bear to go to Dancer's stable. Dancer was looking over the door as if to say, Here I am. Mory went up to her and put her arms around the pony's neck.

"You've *got* to be mine. You've *got* to or I'll die!"

Josh and Cara joined her.

"Only three pounds," said Cara. "If only I'd thought I'd have bought the numnah after the pony sales."

"It makes my money up to twenty-one pounds," said Mory, putting the three pounds in the pocket of her anorak with the rest and doing up the zip. "You're great, both of you."

Sheila and David drove into the yard and Uncle Glyn came out to greet them. The children were waiting by the stables, the ponies looking expectantly over their doors.

"We'd better get them loaded now just in case of trouble," said Uncle Glyn. "We don't want to be late."

Hitching the trailer to the Landrover, he towed it to its usual position against the barn wall and lowered the ramps, front and back.

Cara led Misty from his stable. He walked

calmly up the ramp as he always did.

"We're taking Misty just in case," said Uncle Glyn. "He'll wait happily in the trailer. He's used to it."

With a sinking heart Mory put on Dancer's halter. Her stomach felt like a bottomless pit. Dancer walked up the ramp as quietly as Misty. Mory tied the halter to the twine that was hanging from the ring and patted her.

"This time you're going somewhere," she said, and giving Dancer one last stroke she walked down the front ramp. Uncle Glyn closed it.

"Well, that bit was easy enough," he said.

Dancer gave a whinny. It was the first time she'd been left in the trailer for so long.

"It's all right, Dancer," said Mory, wishing they could go, wishing they could get on with it, wishing it was all over.

They piled into the Landrover and waited for Aunt Olwen, who came panting across the yard.

"It was the telephone," she said. "Sorry. Owen Lewis just checking on us. I told him we were on our way."

Uncle Glyn started the Landrover. There was another long, loud whinny of protest from the trailer as they moved off.

"Give her something to think about now we're going," said Uncle Glyn.

"Stop!" said Cara. "I've forgotten the haynet."

"You'd forget your head if it wasn't screwed on," said Aunt Olwen. The way she said it made everybody laugh except Mory.

Cara ran to the barn and came back with the haynet. She squeezed it into the back.

This time they really were off. Uncle Glyn drove slowly along the lane to the main road. He was careful not to jolt the ponies by driving too fast or braking too suddenly. The drive into Aberdawl took longer than usual and gave everyone time to think. Certainly nobody spoke. Sheila, sitting next to Mory, took hold of the hand Mory was chewing and gently pulled it from her mouth. Mory stared glumly at the bloody thumb.

"I don't care how much it hurts," she thought. "It won't hurt nearly as much as if I lose Dancer."

When they drew into the market square they saw lots of other horse boxes and trailers parked there. Sheila went straight to the chemist to get a plaster for Mory's thumb. Uncle Glyn went to find Owen Lewis, which wasn't difficult as Mr Lewis had been looking out for them. Uncle Glyn lowered the front ramp of the trailer.

"I'll lead Dancer," he said. "Just in case."

Dancer tried to charge out but was held firmly by Uncle Glyn. She held her ears back, alarmed by the strangeness of the market place, the noise and the business which she had never seen before. Mory stroked her neck. Dancer's muscles were straining and tense. Mory was sorrier than ever that she had to go through such an ordeal.

"If only I was rich," she thought. "If only, if only . . . "

Uncle Glyn handed the halter rope to Owen Lewis, who grunted and led Dancer away.

"Not even a word of thanks for looking after his pony," said Aunt Olwen. "That man really is the limit!"

"When will it be time to bid for her?" asked Mory.

"In half an hour or so," said Aunt Olwen.

"Time to do some shopping," said Sheila, "as we're in town."

"I'll stay," said Mory.

"I'll stay with you," said Cara.

"I want to find Dancer."

"This way," said Cara, leading the way towards the cattle pens.

They had no trouble finding Dancer's pen. Owen Lewis was leaning against it, picking his teeth. He spat when they came over but didn't look at them. He was a horrid man. Dancer was beginning to settle. She was growing accustomed to the hustle and bustle going on around her. She came and nuzzled Mory's hand when Mory called to her. Mr Lewis continued to ignore them.

A man, a woman and a girl of about their own age joined him.

"Good morning, Mr Spencer," said Mr Lewis, jumping to attention. "This is the pony I was suggesting you bid for. A nice first pony for your little girl." He grinned a toothy grin at the girl.

"But she's never been ridden," whispered Cara. "How can he know?" Mr and Mrs Spencer and their daughter looked Dancer over.

"She's very pretty," said Mr Spencer.

"Does she bite?" asked the girl.

"A good question, Caroline," said her father. "Does she?"

"No, she doesn't!" said Mory.

Mr and Mrs Spencer and Caroline turned and looked at her. Then they looked away again as if she hadn't spoken. Mory bit her lip. She could have kicked herself for being so stupid.

"She has a kind eye," said Owen Lewis, without a glimpse in Mory's direction. "You can always tell by the eye."

"That doesn't answer my question," said Caroline pertly. "Does she bite?"

"She's never bitten me," said Owen Lewis. Caroline seemed satisfied.

"What do you think, Caroline?" asked Mr Spencer.

"She seems all right," said Caroline, wrinkling her nose. "Is she big enough?"

"Plenty big enough," said Mr Lewis. "You wouldn't want anything bigger just yet. I'd say she was the perfect size."

"All right, Daddy. Buy her," ordered Caroline.

"I'll offer you four hundred for her," said Mr Spencer.

"No, no," said Mr Lewis, looking at the ground and pulling an ear. "I'll not sell her outside of the auction ring. Besides, it's better for you to buy her by bidding. You can have her vetted and you've a forty-eight-hour warranty on her should she prove to be unsound. Not that she is, mind."

Mr and Mrs Spencer strolled off with Mr Lewis, who continued praising Dancer. Caroline was left to push rudely between Mory and Cara.

"Excuse me," she said. "My daddy's going to buy this pony for me." She raised her hand sharply and Dancer backed away.

"Not very friendly, is she? I was going to stroke you, you stupid beast!"

Mory filled with indignation, but before she could say anything Cara pulled her away.

"He's getting those people to bid against us," said Mory. "What happens if that horrid girl gets Dancer? I hate Mr Lewis! I hate him!"

Cara couldn't think of anything comforting to say. The Spencers clearly didn't know the first thing about horses and, unfortunately, looked as if they had lots of money. Cara put her arm firmly through Mory's and led her away. They nearly bumped into Uncle Glyn coming to find them.

"It's time to go in the auction ring," he said. "The bidding for Dancer will start soon."

Cara and Mory followed him between the pens to where the auction took place. Bidding was in progress and people spoke in muted tones against the amplified voice of the auctioneer. A grey pony was being sold.

"I'm bid three fifty, three fifty I'm bid. Three sixty, three sixty, three seventy, three seventy, three eighty. Any improvements on three eighty? A nice little mare. Three eighty, going, going, gone at three hundred and eighty guineas to Mrs Pugh."

The grey pony was led out and another grey pony was led in. The bidding began again and the auctioneer's voice droned on. Mory looked around. She spotted the Spencers. Mr Spencer has his arm around his daughter's shoulder. They were watching the bidding from the opposite side.

Sheila and David came and sat by Mory. Josh, Cara, Uncle Glyn and Aunt Olwen were close. Uncle Glyn leaned over.

"These are the right sort of prices for an unbroken pony," he said. "Around three to four hundred guineas. It'll be interesting to see what we get Dancer for."

The grey pony was sold and Dancer was led in. Mory held her breath.

"Now," said the auctioneer. "Here we have a

nice black mare, a four-year-old, unbroken, but been well handled, excellent mover. What am I bid? Who'll give me two hundred for her?" A woman with a trilby hat nodded and the bidding began. At first it was between the woman and Mr Spencer. At three hundred and twenty guineas the woman dropped out. Uncle Glyn coughed and David began to bid.

"Three hundred and eighty, three hundred and ninety, four hundred." Mory edged nearer to her father. Uncle Glyn looked at Mr Spencer. He didn't know him. He noted that Owen Lewis was behind the auctioneer now.

"Four hundred and fifty, four hundred and sixty." There was a pause while Mr Spencer whispered something to his wife. She nodded.

"Four hundred and sixty. Any offers above four hundred and sixty?" The auctioneer looked hard at Mr Spencer. Mr Spencer nodded. "Four hundred and seventy." David put his hand up. "Four hundred and eighty." Mr Spencer nodded. "Four hundred and ninety." The auctioneer looked at David. David stared at the auctioneer, unable for the moment to shake his head. In an agony of panic Mory unzipped her pocket.

"I've got twenty one pounds," she said. "Enough for five hundred guineas."

"Going, going . . ."

"Five hundred," said David in a loud, clear voice.

"Five hundred guineas I am bid," said the auctioneer, his eyes brightening. He looked at Mr Spencer. Mr Spencer nodded.

"Five hundred and ten guineas I am bid," said the auctioneer looking at David. Slowly David shook his head, "Going, going, gone. Yours sir, for five hundred and ten guineas," said the auctioneer to Mr Spencer. Mr Spencer gave Caroline a hug. Caroline smirked.

"She's got her," moaned Mory.

"I'm sorry, love," said David. "I'm sorry."

Mory bit her lip and her head shrank into her shoulders. Dancer was gone.

NINE

Despair

Nobody knew what to say. Mory felt the loss of Dancer as the keenest disappointment of her life. Something she treasured had been torn from her. She felt numb – too numb even to cry. She could hardly believe they weren't taking Dancer home with them. The family gathered outside the auction ring. David looked shaken and Sheila worried.

"I'd no idea this would happen," said Uncle Glyn. "I've never seen the man we were bidding against before. He'd have just gone on until he got the pony, by the looks of him. Mory, I'm sorry." He put his hand on Mory's arm. Mory looked at her uncle for a moment and then turned and ran for the cattle pens.

"David, stop her," cried Sheila.

Mory reached Dancer's pen before David could stop her. Dancer was gone.

"Where is she?" she yelled.

"It's no use," said David, catching hold of her. "She's gone to someone else. However you feel about it you must accept that she's gone."

"I want to say goodbye!" Mory struggled against her father's grip. David looked round helplessly.

"I don't know where she is," he said. "It's probably too late."

From the corner of her eye Mory caught sight of the girl.

"Over there!" Mory cried. Wriggling like an eel till she was free, she ran between the ponies and people in a mad dash towards where she had seen Caroline Spencer. Mory saw her again at the far end of the car park following Mr Lewis who was leading Dancer.

"Mory, come back!" cried David, dodging recklessly in and out of the passers-by in his effort to stop her. He caught her at last and held her by her coat until he could get his arms around her.

"No, Mory," he said, his breath coming in fast pants. "No, let her go." He felt the fight go out of Mory and she went limp in his arms.

"She's my pony," said Mory. "Mine. She came to me."

"I know that's how you feel," said David. "But you've got to let her go. I'm sure those people will give her a good home and lots of love just as you have done. And though it doesn't seem like it at the moment there will be other ponies."

"There won't be another pony for me," said Mory. She took in a deep, uncontrolled breath, the beginnings of a sob which became a howl of grief.

"Dancer!"

From the other end of the car park came Dancer's long unmistakable whinny in reply. David led the half-stumbling Mory back to the Landrover. Megan and Ian Reece were waiting with the others. Everyone seemed stunned that the auction had ended without them taking Dancer home. It seemed so wrong.

"I think we should go," said Sheila at last. She had her arm around Mory. Mory was about to get in the Landrover, when a horsebox drove past. She knew Dancer was in it when she saw that the car following it had Caroline Spencer sitting in the back. The girl stared at Mory as the car drove past.

"She's my pony!" Mory shouted after her. "She's mine!" Mory was bundled into the Landrover. The girl turned and looked out of the back window. Mory hoped she'd heard.

Uncle Glyn drove the Landrover and trailer out of the car park, leaving Megan and Ian with hands raised in farewell. Nobody spoke. Mory had lost Dancer and no one could bring her back.

When they reached the Llangabby farmyard Mory climbed from the Landrover without a word and began to walk down the track to Black Rock.

"It's rotten," said Josh, as he watched her go. "Really rotten."

"It's funny how things go," said Uncle Glyn.

"That pony was sold for far too much money. Owen Lewis has done himself proud. He set us up, didn't he? Two lots of people who wanted the pony. He's made himself a tidy sum at Mory's expense."

"It seems so cruel," said Aunt Olwen.

"Shall I go after her?" said Sheila.

"I should leave her for a while," said David. "Let her get used to the idea that the pony's gone."

"Poor Mory!" said Cara.

"Well," said Uncle Glyn, "let's get on. We've Misty to unload and I've the sheep to check."

Cara let out a deep sigh and turned to her pony, who had waited so patiently.

It was hard for Mory. Nothing else had been so important before, except for having Splodge. He was the first creature she'd ever had to care for, and Dancer was the second. There had never been any question that Splodge was hers. Why was there this problem with Dancer? Dancer was hers. Dancer knew it too. How could it have happened that these other people had bought her? That girl Caroline would never care for her as she'd done – she wasn't the type.

Mory turned off the track and began to climb the rocky hill overlooking Black Rock Farm. She made herself put one leg in front of the other and keep going. There was no path and the climb was steep, and soon her legs began to ache. She must keep going. One, two. One, two. She saw only the tufted grass, the exposed rock just in front of her eyes. She was going to make herself climb right to the top without stopping. One, two. One, two. Her breath came in urgent gasps. She was weak from lack of food. She used her hands to climb and forced her legs forward, making herself go fast. Her body screamed at her to stop but she wouldn't. Nothing mattered but the climb – not even Dancer.

At the top it was bliss. She lay on her back and let her exhausted body rest. She gazed into the sky. There was a gap of blue between the clouds and Mory stared into it. The heaving in her chest slowly subsided and she breathed more easily.

Gradually the feeling grew in her that Dancer would come back. She didn't know how, but she felt certain she would. Had she read it in the gap in the clouds? She didn't know. Did she have to do something to make it happen? She couldn't say. All she knew for sure was that Dancer would come back. Her whole being knew it. She sat up and looked around. No, there was no one there. No one had told her this.

Mory drew her legs up to her chin and clasped them with her arms. She looked at the view below her. Black Rock Farm lay nestled in the valley. It seemed to welcome her, to want her to return.

This is the worst day of my life, thought Mory. I've lost the one thing I really wanted. She held tight to her knees. But they'll all be down there – Mum, Dad and Josh. They'll be sad too. They wanted me to have Dancer. It came to her that her father wanted his pottery like she wanted Dancer. He'd wanted a pottery for years.

Mory stood up. The certain feeling that Dancer would come back had faded and she no longer felt so confident. She shrugged.

"Maybe Dad's right when he says there are other

ponies," she said aloud, but she knew in a moment that this was wrong. "No," she told the hills. "Not for me. There's only Midnight Dancer for me."

She began her descent. She had to concentrate to stay upright, it was so steep. It would have been easy to stumble. She placed her feet carefully and used what she could as handholds. Jumping the last few feet on to the track, Mory turned into the yard at Black Rock, where she was met by her father.

"You all right?" he asked. Mory nodded. "Come and have something to eat. You haven't eaten all day."

"Okay," Mory said.

In the kitchen, under Sheila's watchful eye, Mory pecked at some salad and ate a hard-boiled egg. Food didn't seem very important somehow and she ate only to please her mother.

Suddenly she fished in her pocket and pulled out her money. She spread it on the table and counted out Josh's eleven pounds fifty pence.

"Here," she said. "You'd better take it in case I spend it."

"Thanks," said Josh. Mory put the rest back in her pocket and reminded herself that she must give Cara back her three pounds.

"I'm starting on the pottery this afternoon," said David. "Anyone want to help?"

"Not me," said Josh. "I'm busy." Mory knew

that he was going up to Llangabby to ride Misty.

"I'll help," she said.

"Thank you, Mory. I'm paying a pound an hour for good, honest, hard work," said David.

"You'd better change into some old clothes then, Mory," said Sheila, ruffling Mory's hair as she went past. Mory went upstairs.

"Ouch!" she said as she bumped her thumb on her bedroom door handle. She wished she hadn't bitten her nail but it was too late now. Pulling on her tattiest pair of jeans and her oldest sweatshirt, the blue one with the frayed cuffs, she looked at the picture of Dancer in the mist. She had drawn it and Dancer had come. She got out her pastels and paper and laid them ready on the table. Tonight she would draw Dancer again. The picture would send a message. The picture would say, Dancer, come home!

David was waiting for her in the kitchen.

"Is my work force ready?" he asked.

"Yup," said Mory.

He led the way into the yard. The sky was throbbing with ominous grey clouds.

"Looks like rain," said Mory.

"It'll be the first for a while," said David. "We've been lucky lately."

The old hen house was to be the pottery. It had been David's dream for a long while to become a full-time potter rather than an art teacher. That was why the offer of Black Rock had been too good an opportunity to miss. The old hen house was a perfect size. It was attached to the side of the farmhouse and was the easiest building to reach from the back door. It meant not getting too wet going from house to pottery if it was raining. He was going to use the cattle stalls as a storehouse for his clay and clay mixer.

David opened the hen house door. The hinges were rusty and the wood rotten. Inside it was gloomy with cobwebs and the windows were so thick with grime that hardly any light shone through.

"Crumbs, Dad!" said Mory. "It's a wreck." She'd already looked all round the cattle stalls, imagined Dancer in one of the stables and thoroughly explored the barn which was on two floors, but she hadn't bothered with the old hen house. It hadn't looked exciting enough.

"It's a wreck now but in a week or so it won't be, you'll see," said David. "The plan is," he went on (and Mory knew he had a plan, for he had been drawing designs for ages), "the plan is to gut it. Everything out, the roof off, floor dug out, damp course, concrete floor, new roof beams, insulated roof and back on with the original tiles which are perfectly good enough. Oh, and bring in electricity. Build an oil-fired kiln at the end and put the oil tank on the outside wall. It'll be in the front garden

but we can grow a creeper over it or something. What do you think?"

"Fine, Dad. Where do we start?"

"That's my girl!" said David. "We start by pulling out all the old bits of wood that can be burned and we pile it in the cattle stalls for the moment."

Mory fetched the wheelbarrow from the barn. When she returned with it David was dragging an old partition towards the door. Sheila joined them and they pulled the partition outside. Mory worked hard, piling wood into the wheelbarrow and trundling it into the cow stalls, where she tipped it out. Sheila worked with a saw and an axe, cutting and chopping the wood into a size that would go into the woodburner.

"I think we should turn the whole house over to oil heating as soon as possible," she said.

"It's not so romantic," said Mory.

"You wait till you've had to hump wood and coal for a whole winter," Sheila said, wielding the axe with a vengeance.

Mory backed her wheelbarrow out as a piece of wood split. She wondered if her mother would let her have a go at chopping. Without meaning to, she let her mind slip to thoughts of Dancer. Where was she now? She must be confused and nervous. It would all be so strange. Mory forced her attention back to the job in hand.

Backwards and forwards she went with the wheelbarrow. The first drops of rain fell and soon it was coming down so hard that David heard it beating on the roof.

"Mory, come inside," he said. "Why didn't you tell me it was raining?"

"I don't mind," said Mory.

"Well, go and fetch your mac. There's no point in getting soaked," said David.

In the kitchen Mory looked at the clock. She'd been working for two and a half hours. Work helped pass the time. Doing things helped keep her mind from worrying about Dancer, although the heavy sense of loss remained with her. It pressed down on her all the time. She paused in the porch by the back door and watched the rain. It reminded her of the day they'd arrived at Black Rock. She felt quite different now, not somewhere strange but somewhere familiar – somewhere she belonged. It would have been perfect if they'd brought Dancer home with them. She barrowed for another half hour and helped Sheila stack the wood.

Hoofbeats in the yard brought them outside to see Cara and Josh leading Misty.

"Uncle Glyn said to put him in our field and give the pony paddock at Llangabby a rest," said Josh.

"Turn him out and then everyone into the kitchen!" said Sheila. "You're all soaked."

Mory gave Misty a soggy pat. He too would be lonely without Dancer. She ran to the gate and opened it. Misty was led in and let go. With ears pricked he looked down the field.

"She's not there, boy," said Mory, patting his neck. To Misty alone she said in a whisper, "If we wish for her hard enough she may come back." Misty plodded forlornly down the field.

Mory wished. She wished that evening in her bedroom as her pastels flew across the paper, conjuring Dancer's image out of black and the paddock out of green and brown. When she was satisfied she pinned the picture beside the other on the wall and climbed into bed.

Suddenly what she had done seemed futile. Drawing a picture! It was useless and silly. Turning out the light, Mory flung herself on her pillow and cried herself to sleep.

TEN

The Lesson

The following morning Mory sat at the kitchen table staring gloomily out of the window. She had slept badly, dreaming of Dancer – Dancer going away, Dancer just out of reach. She managed a piece of toast for breakfast but couldn't bring herself to eat anything more in spite of Sheila's urgings.

When Cara popped her head round the kitchen door Mory was sunk in thought.

"Mory, can you help me get Misty ready? I'm late. I'm going for a riding lesson and Josh and I want you to come too. Only he's doing the sheep with Dad until we go. You'll get to see the Reeces' place. It's great."

"I was going to help Dad," said Mory.

"You go," said Sheila. She looked at David.

"I think I can just about manage without you," said David, smiling. "You have a nice time."

Mory got up from the table with a sigh.

"Okay," she said.

"You just need your wellies and your anorak," said Cara, pushing the door open. Mory absent-mindedly pulled on her anorak in the back porch. Cara put her head back into the kitchen, grinned and gave Sheila and David a brief thumbs-up.

Cara collected Misty from the field and the two girls and the pony walked out of the yard and up the track. They didn't notice Sheila's concerned face watching at the window.

When they turned into the yard at Llangabby Aunt Olwen was hitching up the trailer.

"Hurry up, Cara!" she said. "We need to go in twenty minutes. Where's Josh? He's supposed to be coming too."

"He'll be down in a minute," said Cara. "He went up with Dad on the tractor. Mory, fill a haynet for me please?" she begged. "Mum's getting anxious about the time."

"Yup," said Mory. She went to the tack room and fetched the haynet. She found an already opened bale of hay in the barn and stuffed the net full. She carried it to the Landrover and shoved it in the back.

"Can you give Cara a hand, Mory? She's taking ages," said Aunt Olwen, all of a bustle.

"I already am."

"Good girl. I'll go and see if I can spot Josh."

"What shall I do next?" asked Mory, gently

rubbing Misty behind the ears.

"His mane, please," said Cara. "I'll have a go at his tail. It's a right mess."

Mory rummaged in Cara's grooming box for a mane comb. When she found it she began to tug at the knotty mane. It reminded her of Dancer. First thing that morning she'd gone outside hoping to find her. She'd looked in all sorts of places just in case, but Dancer was nowhere. Somewhere deep inside she'd thought it possible. It was only later, in the cold light of day, that she realised she'd been silly. She thought about the pictures pinned to her wall. They seemed silly too, yet she knew she'd draw another. Drawing seemed the only thing she could do that might help.

At last Misty was ready and Cara loaded him into the trailer.

"Tack!" said Aunt Olwen. Mory ran to fetch it. "Really, that girl is so disorganised!"

Josh came running into the yard at the last minute with Mab at his heels. He clambered into the Landrover and Mab barked around them as they drove out of the yard.

"It's like getting a circus organised, trying to get you lot anywhere on time," grumbled Aunt Olwen. "Have you got your hard hat, Cara?"

"Yes." Cara was sitting with it on her lap.

"Thanks for helping, Mory," said Aunt Olwen. "We'd have been late but for you."

The journey to Megan and Ian's was uneventful. Aunt Olwen drove the Landrover at a steady pace. Mory, sitting in the front next to her, stayed silent while Cara and Josh told jokes in the back. The Landrover engine made hearing them difficult and Mory didn't try. They stayed on single-track lanes for most of the way and she wondered what they would do if they met anything coming the other way. They didn't – the lanes were deserted. It made Mory realise how scantily populated this part of Wales was, so unlike the busy town of Waring and the fast, wide roads of Surrey.

The lane they were in came to an end at a junction with a two-lane road.

"Nearly there," said Aunt Olwen. She waited for a tractor to chug past before pulling out, then signalled almost immediately to turn left. Beyond some trees Mory could make out a stone house with large outbuildings. They turned into a driveway where a sign announced *Penyworlod Equestrian Centre*.

Aunt Olwen pulled up by the side of a large building in what appeared to be a car park. Other cars were parked nearby, along with a trailer and horsebox.

"This is the indoor school," said Cara, nodding at the building they were next to. "It's big."

Mory was curious. She hadn't really thought about horses going about indoors before. Cara, full of enthusiasm, had Misty unloaded and tacked up in no time, helped by Josh. Misty knew the routine and was no trouble.

"Come on," said Cara, leading Misty round the end of the indoor school. "This way." Josh followed.

"She's forgotten her hat," said Aunt Olwen.

"I'll take it," said Mory.

"I'll be right with you. I'm going to put the front ramp up in case it gets in anyone's way," said Aunt Olwen.

Mory was about to follow the others when a car pulled into the car park. She would have thought nothing of it but for the face she saw looking out of the window. It was the girl, Caroline Spencer. Mory's heart seemed to leap in her chest. She watched the girl get out of the car. There was no mistaking, it was her. Mory hurried after the others.

On the other side of the indoor school was a big fenced-off area. Cara led Misty into it and Megan joined her. Megan said a few words and Cara put her hand to her head. Mory held up the hat.

"I've got it!" she shouted. Mory walked around the fence to the gate.

"Thanks, Mory," said Cara. She pulled on her hat and did up the strap.

"How are you today, Mory?" asked Megan.

"Fine, thank you," said Mory.

"This is the outdoor school," said Cara. "There's

a beginners' lesson going on inside so I'm going to bc out hcrc."

"Where's Josh?" asked Mory.

"He's joining the beginners. Would you like to?' asked Megan. "We can soon find you a pony."

"No, thanks," said Mory. Her eye caught sight of Caroline Spencer walking from the car park with her father. Aunt Olwen was following behind them, looking in her handbag. Mory didn't think she knew who they were.

"Crumbs!" said Cara. "It's –!" She stopped and looked at Mory.

"I already saw her," said Mory. Mory could tell

from Megan's face that she recognised the girl too and was as surprised as they were.

"Excuse me a moment," she said, and hurried over to the Spencers.

Mory and Cara watched as Megan shook Mr Spencer by the hand and said hello to Caroline. She pointed towards what Mory assumed were the stables and the two of them walked in that direction. Megan waited for Aunt Olwen and they chatted briefly before Megan followed the Spencers.

'What's *she* doing here?" said Cara. Mory didn't care. All she wanted was news of Dancer.

"Well, that's a turn-up for the book!" said Aunt Olwen, joining them. "That's Caroline Spencer, the girl who has Dancer."

"We know," said Cara.

"She's come to join the beginners' class."

"Crumbs! She's a beginner and she's got Dancer. Her dad must be mad," said Cara.

"Well, I'm a beginner and I was going to have her," said Mory.

"You're different," said Cara. "You've got a way with you."

Mory was touched by the compliment. She and Dancer did get on, she knew that. It was hard to imagine Caroline Spencer doing the same.

"Will I be able to watch the beginners' lesson?" she asked.

"You can if you like," said Cara. "There's a

coffee bar upstairs where you can look down, or you can sit in the arena at the far end."

A trail of ponies arrived at the big doors of the indoor school. Josh was on a chestnut pony. He waved. Ian opened the doors and Josh led the way into the school. Caroline joined the end of the ride on a bay pony led by her father. She smacked his hand away and kicked the pony into the school.

"Crumbs!" said Cara for the second time.

Mory's spirits sank at the thought of a spoiled brat like that owning Dancer. Megan shut the doors and came over.

"What an extraordinary thing!" she said. "It was Mr Spencer who bought Dancer yesterday."

"Why did they have to come here?" said Cara.

"Mr Spencer told me when he rang that they'd purchased an unbroken pony for his daughter. He said she wanted to get on it as soon as possible. But the name meant nothing to me when he booked."

"Is Dancer all right?" asked Mory.

"She's in their paddock and they haven't done anything with her yet. They've recently moved here, Mr Spencer said, and as soon as they arrived Caroline asked for a pony. Having bought the pony Mr Spencer thought she'd better have some lessons. She's only ridden once or twice before."

"Honestly!" said Cara. "They don't know the first thing about anything."

"Well, let's get on, Cara," said Megan. "Walk

Misty around and get him loosened up."

Mory went to watch Josh and found her way into the spectators' part of the school. She sat herself as far away as possible from Mr Spencer, who was beaming encouragement. There were five pupils in the class including Josh and Caroline. Mory wondered if Josh recognised Caroline from the auction, but he didn't seem to.

It was interesting watching. Josh was enjoying the chestnut pony and developed a good relationship with him as the lesson progressed. Caroline Spencer got crosser and crosser with her pony. Mory tried to work out if the pony wasn't doing what it was told because it didn't want to, or whether Caroline was upsetting it by the way she pulled it this way and that.

"Use your legs, Caroline," Ian said over and over again. Mory hoped Caroline would be more sensitive with Dancer. Watching made her depressed, so she left.

In the outdoor arena Cara and Misty were doing well. Misty was walking straight with his head turned away from the direction he was going. Mory wondered how Cara asked him to do it.

"Is that easy?" she asked Aunt Olwen, who was leaning over the rail watching.

"Don't ask me," said her aunt. "All I know is that it's called 'shoulder in'. You'll have to ask Cara how she does it."

The lesson in the school came to an end and the class came out leading their ponies. Caroline Spencer went with the others back to the stables. Josh led his pony over to them. He was grinning from ear to ear.

"This is Rustler," he said. "Ian wants to know if you'd like a go on him, Mory. Do ride him. He's super."

Josh unfastened his hat and offered it. Mory was going to say no when she suddenly felt a strong urge to ride well for Dancer's sake. She put on the hat.

"Bring him in here," said Megan. "We're finished now."

Mory rode Rustler into the outdoor school. He felt quite different from Misty. He had a quickness about him that almost took her by surprise. He was keen to go forwards like Misty, which she liked.

"Trot him on round," said Megan.

Mory asked Rustler to trot and found herself able to respond to the rhythm of the pony with a stable up-and-down, up-and-down rising trot. She was really pleased with herself. Stopping, she patted Rustler's neck and smiled.

"He's very nice, isn't he?" she said.

"I'm glad you like him," said Ian, who had joined the others at the rail. "You can take him home with you if you like."

"Yes, please!" said Josh. "Yes, please!"

"It's called having a pony on trial," said Megan. Mory's heart sank.

"But I don't want Rustler," she thought. "I want Dancer." Then she realised, He's for Josh! That made her glad they were taking Rustler home with them.

"Come on, let's go!" cried Josh. He could hardly wait.

ELEVEN

Into The Hills

Rustler loaded easily into the trailer. He waited for Misty to go in and followed happily. He seemed as used to travelling as his companion. The ponies shared the haynet that Cara tied up for them, munching contentedly.

"Megan," said Mory shyly when no one else could overhear, "if they tell you what's happening with Dancer, will you tell me?"

"I'll pass on any news I hear," promised Megan. "I hope you get on well with Rustler. He's a really nice pony."

"Josh is potty about him already," said Mory. "I know he'll want him if he can have him." Megan didn't reply. Goodbyes were said and Aunt Olwen drove the Landrover out of the car park. The Spencers' car had already gone.

"It's a super place, isn't it?" said Cara.

"It's great," said Mory. "I'd like to come again."

Back home in the Llangabby yard Aunt Olwen lowered the ramps on the trailer.

"You can walk the ponies down to Black Rock." she said. "It's too bumpy to take the trailer down."

"Where are you going, Josh?" called Mory, when she saw Josh disappearing out of the yard. Josh looked embarrassed.

"I was going to find Uncle Glyn," he said awkwardly.

"Come on," said Mory. "You wanted him. You take Rustler down." Josh looked helplessly at Aunt Olwen.

"Don't you want to?" asked Mory.

"Of course I do," said Josh.

"Well, go on then," said his sister. "Daft-head!" Reluctantly Josh untied Rustler's halter rope and led him down the front ramp. Cara followed with Misty.

"I'll clear out the trailer," volunteered Mory.

"No, Mory," said Aunt Olwen. "I'll do it. You go down with the others and get to know Rustler."

Josh and Cara led the ponies down the track side by side. Mory walked slightly ahead of them.

"It's all gone wrong," Josh whispered to Cara. "She thinks he's for me." He was torn between wanting Mory to want Rustler and knowing that he wanted him himself, which was not what was supposed to happen at all. "The trouble with secret plans is that they don't always go how you expect," he said.

Mory opened the field gate and the two ponies were led in.

"I think he's great, Josh. Fancy Megan and Ian letting you have him just like that!" she said.

"But Mory, he's supposed to be for *you*, not me!" Josh burst out. "He's to make up for not getting Dancer."

"But I don't want him! I really don't want him!"

"We could share him," said Josh. He looked desperate.

"Okay," said Mory. "We'll share him. But if I ever get the chance I want Dancer back."

"But if you don't say you want Rustler he'll have to go back," said Josh.

"This is silly. I'm going to talk to Mum and Dad," said Mory, marching off.

Mory and her parents were sitting round the kitchen table when Josh and Cara came in.

"I've explained," said Mory. "About not wanting a different pony."

"You're right," said Sheila. "It was a silly idea. Only Megan told Aunt Olwen she had a perfect pony. It was worth a try."

"Josh thinks he's great, and Rustler's here now. I think Josh should try him out," said Mory. "But if I could ever have Dancer back I'd want her. Not a different pony, never ever."

"Well, this is a dilemma," said David. "Leave it with me and Mum. We'll have a think about it. You can both ride Rustler for the time being."

"Great!" said Mory. "Tomorrow we can take the

ponies out into the hills. I don't mind walking."

"We can do doublers some of the way on Misty," said Cara.

"And take it in turns on Rustler," said Josh, feeling guilty and pleased at the same time.

It was agreed. They planned to leave the following morning about eleven o'clock, which would give them time to make a picnic and get the ponies ready.

"It's time we went into the hills," said Mory. "I want to have a really good look at Wales."

"We can go fairly high," said Cara. "The highest mountains are furthest away. We won't have time to reach them. We could ask Mum to drive us there one day."

"No," said Mory. "When I'm a really good rider I shall ride up." And to herself she added, on Dancer, if she comes back.

The following morning everything was shrouded in a fine mist. Mory turned from her bedroom window, where she had been inspecting the weather prospects, and looked at the pictures on the wall. There were three now. Mory had drawn another of Dancer looking over her stable door. Three pictures of Dancer seemed just right. Come back soon, she wished.

It was nice and early. Mory went outside and wondered if the mist would clear or if it was going to turn into one of those drizzly days. It didn't matter, she decided – they were going anyway. She collected the headcollars and went to the field, where Josh joined her at the gate. They caught the ponies and brought them round to the stables, gave them some pony nuts and left them to dry off.

In the kitchen Mory made cheese sandwiches.

Josh washed some apples and found a packet of chocolate biscuits, then poured orange juice into a plastic beaker with a watertight lid.

"And where are you going on this picnic?" Sheila asked.

"Not far," said Mory. "Just into the hills."

"I hope the weather clears," said Sheila dubiously. "I don't want you getting lost."

"Cara knows where we're going. Don't worry, Mum," said Mory.

"The mist is clearing anyway," said Josh. He was right. A weak sun was breaking through. "I expect it means it's going to be a hot day after all," he added.

"It jolly well should be," said Mory. "It's rained enough."

When Cara came down she brought more goodies – hard-boiled eggs, tomatoes and some flapjacks for pudding.

"I made the flapjacks," she said.

They packed the picnic into Josh's knapsack and collected waterproofs just in case.

"We're off!" called Mory.

Sheila came into the kitchen.

"I'll expect you back by four. Have you got a watch?" Mory waved her wrist in the air displaying her Mickey Mouse watch.

"Have a nice time," said Sheila. She disappeared back to whatever she was doing, leaving them free to go.

They crossed the yard to the stables and set to work on the ponies. When they were ready they were led outside.

"I'll take the rucksack on Misty," said Cara. "We can tie it on with baler twine."

"Here's some," said Mory, rummaging in her pocket.

The rucksack secured, they led the ponies onto the track.

"Megan and Ian are great," said Mory, "letting us try Rustler and lending us all the gear."

"I could have told you that," said Cara, mounting Misty.

Josh mounted Rustler and the ponies led the way. Mory felt a twinge of loss. She might have been riding Dancer into the hills for the first time if all had gone well. How she wished she were! She pushed the wish away and followed the others.

The track led downhill. As the land opened out it narrowed until it was only a sheep path. The mist obscured the wonderful view Cara assured them was there.

"One day we'll see it," said Mory.

They stopped to tighten girths. The path swung away to the right and began to go uphill. Misty led the way.

"It'll take us to a track at the top," said Cara. "We can follow it right into the hills."

The higher they went, the less dense the mist

became. At last they came into sunshine. Looking back they saw Black Rock Farm floating in a sea of mist.

"Your turn," said Cara, sliding off Misty. She gave Mory a leg-up. "Why don't you trot on? Wait for me at the top of the slope."

Cara watched the ponies trot ahead. Mory concentrated on rising up and down to the rhythm of the trot. She was getting much better at it. At the top they waited till Cara arrived, puffing and hot. She flung herself to the ground and followed the flight of a large bird gliding above her. It mewed a plaintive call.

"A buzzard!" Cara panted. The others looked up.

"It's huge," said Mory, taking in the bird's effortless glide.

"You get lots of them round here," said Cara.

Rustler stamped a foot impatiently, wanting to go. In the distance, beyond the top of the next hill, a thin trickle of smoke rose up.

"Let's go towards the smoke," Josh said.

They took a sheep track which led them into a dip full of heather. At the bottom it was boggy. The ponies' feet sank into the ooze. Cara, wearing jodhpur boots, had to pick her way across.

"Hang on, Cara," said Mory. "Let's do a doubler on Misty." Misty obligingly waded back to fetch his owner. Cara vaulted onto his back and held

Mory's waist. Misty didn't seem to mind carrying them both. He squelched to the end of the muddy bit. Josh found a path and Rustler led the way up.

At the top of the hill they looked down onto a small stone house with smoke coming from its chimney. Cara slid off Misty and walked.

The sheep track went down and joined a vehicle track which ended in front of the house. A man was working in the back garden, partly hidden by apple trees. He didn't look up and didn't see them. They joined the vehicle track and followed it towards the house. As they came closer, the track swung round and they saw a battered, blue car parked by the front gate. Mory tried to remember where she'd seen the car before.

Josh trotted Rustler on ahead. It was a flat and inviting stretch of ground, so inviting that Rustler took it into his head to go faster and broke into a canter.

"Wait, Josh!" cried Mory. As she cried out the man appeared suddenly at the front door. Rustler shied sharply and Josh tumbled over his shoulder.

"Let me take Misty," said Cara. "I'll catch Rustler. You see if Josh is all right." Rustler trotted some distance from the house and began to graze.

Mory ran to help. Josh clambered to his feet and began to brush himself down.

"Are you all right?" she asked.

"I'm fine," said Josh. "That's the first fall over

with." He grinned. "One down, goodness knows how many to go!"

The man marched over to them before they could move away. Mory almost jumped out of her skin. It was Mr Lewis.

"What do you want?" he said. "Spying on me, I suppose?"

"No, we weren't," said Mory. For some reason her eyes slid past Mr Lewis and looked into the back of his car. On the back seat was a pile of pony tack.

"Clear off!" said Mr Lewis. "Go on, clear off! I won't have kids spying on me or I'll let the dog

off." As if to emphasise his point a dog barked loudly from inside the house.

Mory and Josh went. Neither of them ran but they walked purposefully towards Cara, who was holding the ponies. Mr Lewis followed them a few steps.

"Go on!" he shouted. "Clear off!"

Josh remounted Rustler.

"That's something you'd better watch. Rustler's liable to bunk off with you," said Cara. "Be ready to hold him back. Better get up on Misty, Mory, just in case Mr Lewis does let the dog off."

"That must have been old Mr Lewis's place," said Mory.

"It is," said Cara. "I wasn't going to mention it. It was stupid of me not to realise that Owen Lewis might be there."

Mory looked back. Mr Lewis watched them go and shook his fist.

"Let's get away from here," Mory said, afraid of what Mr Lewis might do next. Cara and Josh urged the ponies forward and they trotted up the hill and away from the house.

TWELVE

The Rescue

The children were upset by their meeting with Mr Lewis. Of course they hadn't spied on him. Why ever should they do that? Luckily the cloud he had cast over them soon evaporated. They came to a hollow between two ridges, which looked an inviting place for a picnic, and dismounted. Taking turns, they held the ponies while they grazed on the scrubby grass between the heather.

The cheese sandwiches, the eggs and the tomatoes were soon eaten. The apples were given to the ponies. They were starting on the flapjacks when the sun went behind a large grey cloud.

"Oh, no!" said Cara. She'd meant to be on guard for bad weather.

"It's going to rain again," said Mory. "The weather here's bananas!"

"It does change quickly. Dad told me the weather forecast said rain later. I was supposed to be watching out for it. Now we're going to get soaked."

"Let's swig the orange juice and start back," said

Josh. He took a quick drink and handed it to Cara. Mory held the ponies while Josh and Cara tightened their girths. Mory drank the last of the juice and packed the knapsack.

"At least we brought our waterproofs just in case," she said, putting hers on.

They turned the ponies for home. Mory took first turn with Rustler. She stroked his chestnut neck. When they got to the top of the ridge they felt the wind. Walking into it made the going harder. By the time they turned down the track that led to old Mr Lewis's house it had come on to rain really hard.

"I don't suppose Mr Lewis'd let us shelter until it stops," shouted Mory.

"I don't think it's going to stop," cried Cara. "The sooner we get home the better. They'll start worrying about us if we don't."

"They won't start to worry yet," said Mory.

"They will because of the rain," said Josh, leaning into the wind and walking doggedly on.

They came nearer to the house – the two ponies, their riders and the walking figure bent into the rain, soaked and bedraggled. Mr Lewis's dog was barking. It was an urgent bark for which they could see no reason. They were startled by a shout.

"Quick!" cried Cara, "he's seen us."

"No," said Mory. "Listen." The shout came again. Someone was calling, she was sure of it. The dog barked louder.

"I'm going to see what's the matter," Mory said.

"I'll come with you," said Cara. "Josh, can you manage both ponies?"

"I'll try," said Josh.

Mory dismounted and handed over the hat. Josh climbed on to Rustler's back. The ponies stood forlornly in the pouring rain, their heads hanging. Josh sat hunched on Rustler, holding Misty.

As the girls neared the back door the cry came

again. Someone was in distress. Mory knocked on the door and the barking became a frenzy. She pushed the door. It was stiff but it gave, catching on the floor beneath. Inside an Alsatian was tied to the leg of a stout oak table. The dog growled and crouched as if to spring. There was no one in the room.

"Hello," said Mory. The dog barked again.

"I'm over here!" The voice sounded hoarse and tired.

They found Mr Lewis in a passageway, lying in a crumpled heap on the floor.

"I was hoping you'd hear me," he said. He was surrounded by blankets at the foot of a wooden staircase. Judging by where he was lying, he must have fallen down it. "I think my ankle's broken," he said. "I can't get up."

"We'll go for help," said Mory.

"Can't one of you stay?" asked Mr Lewis. "I could get up if I had a shoulder to lean on." Mory didn't want to stay, yet she knew she couldn't refuse when the man was injured and helpless.

"I'll stay," she said.

"I can't leave you here," Cara said.

"You'll have to. You and Josh go for help on the ponies. You both ride better than me. I'd only hold you up. Go on." Mory more or less pushed Cara out of the front door and watched as she told Josh. She could see Josh arguing and ran out to them.

"You've got to go, Josh. You've got to get the ponies home and get help for Mr Lewis. I'll be all right." Josh's teeth were chattering. "Go on," said Mory. "If you get going you'll warm up."

She watched the ponies trot along the track out of sight and ran back to the house. The dog growled as she came in. Keeping well away from it she went to Mr Lewis.

"Help me up," he commanded.

"I don't think I should," said Mory, trying hard to remember her first aid. "You shouldn't be moved but you should be made comfortable." Mory collected the scattered blankets as a prelude to achieving some comfort for the man on the floor. There wasn't much room. She could see why he would prefer to move. Carefully Mory lifted the blankets from Mr Lewis's legs. The top leg looked all right but the foot of the leg underneath was bent at an odd angle.

"Help me straighten up," said Mr Lewis.

"We must do it slowly," said Mory, looking at Mr Lewis's face, which was grey with pain. "Before we try let me lay some blankets on the floor. When help comes they'll be able to lift you like on a stretcher if I do them thick enough."

Mr Lewis watched as she chose two of the thickest blankets and folded them in half. She lay one on top of the other. Mory thought they would be strong enough to take the weight.

"I think I should try and splint your ankle," she said. "If it's held in position it'll be less painful when you move."

"You'll find some pieces of firewood out the back," said Mr Lewis. "You'll have to rip up a sheet to tie them with. There's some upstairs. Only for goodness' sake don't do what I did and trip!"

"I won't," said Mory.

"I was daft. Trying to carry too much," said Mr Lewis, nodding towards the blankets. "More haste less speed. But the house had got to be cleared. The owner wants to sell it, you see."

Mory squeezed past Mr Lewis, taking care not to bump his leg. In the back room she found a pile of wood stacked along a wall and chose a piece of planking. If she could get it under the ankle she could strap the ankle to the plank. She stepped over Mr Lewis and went upstairs. There were two bedrooms. One was empty, but in the other she found a bed and a chest of drawers. There was a pile of sheets on the bed. She chose the oldest and went downstairs.

"Can you turn over if I support your shoulders from the back?" Mory asked.

"I'll try," said Mr Lewis. Mory got down on her knees behind him. Slowly, bit by bit, Mr Lewis turned himself over and lay biting his lip. Mory rolled up a blanket and put it behind his head, then laid the plank beside his leg. She tore the sheet into strips and put four strips under the plank to act as ties.

"This is the worst bit," she said. "I'm going to move your leg on to the plank. I'll be as gentle as I can."

Slowly she lifted the leg, supporting the foot with one hand. It was heavy. Mr Lewis held his breath and grunted. At last his leg lay on the plank.

"I think you should take my shoe off," he said. "For the swelling."

"Should I? I don't know," said Mory. "But if you want me to I will."

"Go on," said Mr Lewis.

Mory undid the laces and loosened them as much as she could. The foot had swollen above the shoe. She pulled.

"It won't come."

"It's got to," said Mr Lewis through clenched teeth. "Try again."

He braced himself. Mory hated to hurt him but she pulled harder, easing the shoe until it came off. Mr Lewis let out a long breath as it did so.

"That was brave," said Mory.

"I got no choice, have I?" he said.

Mory tied the sheets around the plank and Mr Lewis's ankle and shin.

"Now I can lift your leg more easily," she said. "If you can wriggle the rest of your body on to the blankets, you'll be ready to go when help comes."

Mr Lewis manoeuvred himself on to the blankets with his good leg and his arms, while Mory held the splinted leg. It didn't take as long as she'd thought it would. As soon as he was lying down comfortably she covered him with the remaining blankets.

"Thank you," he muttered. Moving had been painful. There was nothing to do now but sit and wait. The dog stirred in the other room and whined.

"Quiet, Scout!" said Mr Lewis.

The dog was quiet. Mory sat hunched against the wall. She hoped the others had got back safely and that help wouldn't be too long in coming. She was getting very cold. The light grew dimmer and the rain pelted against the window.

* * *

They stayed like that for what seemed like ages. Mory heard the dog stir and looked at her watch. Seeing was difficult in the gloom. She thought it said half past four. She wanted to ask Mr Lewis if she could turn on the light, but he seemed to be asleep.

The rain lashed the window in several gusts and the dog began to bark. Mr Lewis grunted. At last Mory heard voices. She staggered to her feet as the front door opened.

"We're back here," she said, her voice coming out in a sob. She got a grip on herself as David came into the room.

"Mory!" he said. "Are you all right?" Uncle Glyn and Aunt Olwen followed.

"I'm fine," said Mory, noticing that she was trembling all over. "It's Mr Lewis. He's broken his ankle."

She wished she could stop shivering. Shc found herself enveloped in a blanket and Aunt Olwen's arms about her. Mory heard Uncle Glyn's voice.

"What are we going to do about the dog, Owen? He's a vicious blooming thing."

"He'll do as he's told. Keep him on the lead and be firm with him," said Mr Lewis.

"The things I do!" said Uncle Glyn. "First we'd better get you in the Landrover."

It was a bumpy ride back to Black Rock Farm. Aunt Olwen sat with Mory in the front and David sat with Mr Lewis and the dog in the back. The ride must have hurt Mr Lewis a lot but he didn't say anything. At Black Rock Aunt Olwen ushered Mory out of the Landrover and into the house. Uncle Glyn and David drove off with Mr Lewis and the dog.

"They're taking him to the hospital at Aberdawl," she said. "He'll be fine."

Once indoors, Mory was taken by Sheila to the bathroom, stripped of her wet clothes and ordered into a hot bath. The others had to wait to hear what had happened.

It was only when they were sitting round the kitchen table that Mory was allowed to tell her tale. When she finished Sheila spoke.

"What an extraordinary thing!" she said. "I'm proud of you all for going to the rescue like that. Well done!"

"Are the ponies all right?" asked Mory.

"They're fine," said Cara. "I think they rather enjoyed their adventure."

"We came back really fast," said Josh. "We cantered some of the way. It was great."

"Rustler was really good," said Cara.

"So we've got to keep him, Mum. We've got to," said Josh.

"We'll see," said Sheila. "Both my children have gone pony mad. Is there no end to it?" she laughed.

THIRTEEN

Birthday Surprise

Mory awoke to her birthday. No one had mentioned it the day before and she'd hardly thought about it herself. She absent-mindedly stroked Splodge and tickled his tummy until he boxed her hand with his legs and jumped off the bed, stretched a long, satisfying cat stretch and walked to the door. Sighing, Mory pulled back the duvet and heaved herself out of bed.

Downstairs in the kitchen Sheila was making tea.

"Happy birthday my lovely," she said. "Where are your slippers?"

"Don't fuss, Mum, it's not cold," said Mory.

"That's what parents are for," said Sheila. "To fuss. I thought you'd know that by now, especially as you're so old."

Mory opened the back door and Splodge trotted outside with his tail in the air. The day smelt fresh and was going to be sunny after yesterday's rain.

"Close the door," said Sheila. "It's chilly."

"How's Mr Lewis?" asked Mory. She and Josh

had been in bed long before David came home.

"A broken ankle as you suspected. You were commended on your splint, by the way."

"Did he have to stay in hospital?"

"No," said Sheila. "Dad and Uncle Glyn waited with Mr Lewis's wife and took them both home. That was why they were so late. Now go upstairs and get dressed. Birthday breakfast coming up."

"Oh, Mum!"

"Go on," said Sheila.

Mory's favourite breakfast was fried egg and mushrooms on fried bread. She wasn't allowed to have it very often as her parents said it was too fatty. She hoped she'd have enough appetite to eat it – food still didn't interest her much.

By the time she was washed and dressed the whole family was assembled in the kitchen. The table was set and there were cards and two parcels by her place.

"Happy birthday!" chorused Josh and David.

"Thanks," said Mory, sitting down.

"Cards and presents," said Josh. "Come on, hurry up and open them!"

There were cards from Josh, from her parents, from Aunt Olwen and Uncle Glyn, from Cara and from her friend Hannah in Surrey. This last card gave Mory's memory a jolt and she made a mental note to start a letter to her friend as soon as possible. She arranged the cards on the window-sill as the eggs spluttered in the frying pan.

"Breakfast is ready," said David, getting warmed plates from the oven.

"Quick! The presents!" said Josh. "The big one's from Mum and Dad and the little one's from me."

Mory opened the big one first. She pulled off the wrapping paper and found a brand new jockey skull cap. She put it on.

"Does it fit properly?" Sheila asked. "We can change it if it doesn't." Mory did up the strap. The strap needed adjusting but the skull cap fitted perfectly.

"Thank you. It's great," she said. "Now we won't have to keep swopping hats all the time." She opened the little present and found a black and red silk to go on the hat.

"Thanks, Josh," she said. "I'll look really smart in this."

"Clear the table! Clear the table!" said David, hovering with a plate of food in each hand. He put one in front of Mory and the other in front of Josh. Sheila put two more plates on the table and the eating began.

They had just about finished when the sound of running feet made them turn their heads towards the back door. It was Cara.

"Mum's had a phone call from Mrs Lewis, Owen Lewis's wife. She wants you all to go and see them today about something important."

"Did she say what?" asked Sheila.

"No, but she said it had to be today as soon as you could manage," said Cara.

"Now what?" said David. He wanted to work on the pottery without any more interruptions. Yesterday had been bad enough.

"It's a bit odd," said Sheila.

"Maybe Mr Lewis wants to thank Mory in person," said Josh.

"Maybe he does," said David. "But it doesn't have to be today, does it? Oh well, I suppose we'd better go. Perhaps breaking his ankle has made him demented."

"David!" said Sheila.

"Sorry, Mr Lewis."

"Thanks for my card," said Mory.

"Oh," said Cara. "I forgot in the rush. Happy birthday, Mory!"

An hour later the Harper family car, driven by Sheila, was heading for Aberdawl. Mory, Josh and Cara sat expectantly in the back. David grumbled in the front.

"This is probably a complete waste of time," he moaned. "I wanted to get on."

"Don't worry, Dad. I'll help when we get back," said Mory.

"Thank you, Mory," said David. "*If* we ever get back."

They drove into the outskirts of Aberdawl.

"Start directing me, David," Sheila said. "You know where the house is."

"I'll try and remember," said David. They went wrong only once and at last Sheila pulled up in front of a terraced house with a blue front door.

The family assembled on the pavement and David knocked. The door was opened by a woman who was all smiles.

"This is Mrs Lewis," said David. Mrs Lewis shook hands with Sheila.

"And you must be Mory," she said and Mory blushed. "Come in, come in. Here am I keeping you on the doorstep. He's in the front room through here."

Mr Lewis sat close to a gas fire with his plastered foot on a stool. Leaning against the chair was a pair of crutches.

"Morning, Owen!" said David. "How's the foot?"

"Fine," said Mr Lewis. He couldn't look any of them in the eye.

"Sit down now," said Mrs Lewis, and they arranged themselves on the sofa and the variety of chairs the room had to offer.

Mory looked around in the pause that followed. She was surprised to see a saddle and bridle on the floor behind Mr Lewis's chair.

"It's been a busy morning," said Mrs Lewis, making conversation to fill the gap. "My neighbour took me to fetch home the car. Now that's all sorted, thank goodness."

"It must have been a shock for you," said Sheila.

"I was wondering where he'd got to when your husband and Glyn Morgan arrived. It was kind of them to take me to the hospital and bring us back."

There was another pause. Mr Lewis cleared his throat.

"I had a phone call this morning," he said at last. "From the people who bought that pony you wanted. They don't want to keep her."

Mory's heart almost leapt into her mouth. She sat rigid on the edge of her seat.

"They say I should take her back under the forty-eight-hour guarantee. I asked if there was anything wrong with her and they said she was bad tempered."

Dancer bad tempered? Mory was shocked. If Dancer had done something wrong they must have done something to cause it.

"Apparently she kicked the girl or bit her," Mr Lewis continued. "I don't know what. Anyway, I said that was no reason for me to have her back. I only have to take her if she's unsound. I said to leave it with me as I thought I knew someone who would like her. I got their address."

"That's when I rang you," said Mrs Lewis. "Owen told me about your daughter wanting the pony."

"That's the situation," said Mr Lewis. "You can

buy the pony from them if you want."

"For how much?" asked David.

"That's between you and them," said Mr Lewis. "I expect they'll be reasonable. They want to get rid of it."

"Can we go now?' said Mory, her eyes shining.

"May I use your phone and give them a ring?" Sheila asked. "I feel we should talk to them first."

"Of course you can," said Mrs Lewis. "It's in the hall. I'll put the kettle on."

David and Sheila followed Mrs Lewis. The children sat uncomfortably. There was a long silence, broken suddenly by Mr Lewis.

"It's a fine old pickle I'm in!" he muttered

crossly, pointing to his broken ankle. "Stuck in a chair for weeks, I am."

"Does it hurt much?" Cara asked politely.

"It hurts," said Mr Lewis. "It'll teach me to be more blooming careful in future, won't it?" He scratched the back of his neck.

Mory sat thinking of Dancer. Dancer, poor Dancer! She hoped beyond hope the Spencers would sell her to them.

"Please, please, let them!" she wished. She sat in an agony of suspense. She could hear her mother talking but she couldn't make out what was said.

Mrs Lewis came in with a loaded tray: cups of tea for the grown-ups, orange juice for the children and chocolate biscuits. Mory heard her mother say goodbye and put the phone down. Her parents talked to one another in the hall for what seemed like ages before they came in. Sheila smiled at her daughter's anxious face.

"I've made some tea," said Mrs Lewis, handing round the cups. "Now, Owen," she said, nodding to her husband.

"We've agreed a price," said Sheila.

"That *is* good news," said Mrs Lewis.

"Does that mean Dancer is mine?" asked Mory.

"It does!" said David.

The joy and the relief made Mory leap to her feet! She wanted to go. She wanted to fetch Dancer that very instant. It was hard to have to sit down and wait while the grown-ups drank their tea.

"Owen," said Mrs Lewis again. Prompted for the second time Mr Lewis cleared his throat.

"Behind my chair is a saddle and bridle," he said. "It's for the pony. A thank-you for helping me yesterday." He almost managed to look at Mory. Mory stood up. "Well, take it," he said.

"Thank you very much," said Mory. She picked up the saddle and bridle and stood not knowing what to do.

"We must go," said Sheila. She put her cup on the tray. "It's very kind of you to give Mory the saddle and bridle and thank you for telling us about the pony."

"One good turn," said Mrs Lewis. Mr Lewis, clearly embarrassed, said nothing.

As they drove off Mory was half-laughing, half-crying.

"This is the best day of my life! Can we fetch her straight away? Please can we?"

"We've got to go to the bank and collect some money," said David.

"How much have we got to pay?" asked Josh.

"Four hundred pounds," said David.

"*Four* hundred pounds?" said Mory. "But that's over a hundred pounds less than they paid for her."

"Your mum's very good at bargaining. Besides, the pony's got vices. It kicks."

"She's never kicked me," said Mory.

"They seemed happy with the price," said Sheila.

"Only too glad to get rid of what turned out to be a mistake," said David. "So all's well that ends well."

"*And* I've got a saddle and a bridle! It's my lucky day!" yelled Mory.

"Watch the decibels, please," said David. "And just remember your poor old dad needs lots of help with the pottery. The sooner I can make pots the sooner I can sell them."

"I'll help, Dad. You know I will," said Mory.

"And I will," said Josh.

After the visit to the bank the car sped them back to Llangabby. Aunt Olwen and Uncle Glyn were told the news and Cara was sent off to fetch Misty.

"Best make it the easiest journey possible," said Aunt Olwen.

Josh filled a haynet and Mory hopped from one leg to the other impatiently as the trailer was hitched up. Then, at the last minute, she rushed to the tack room and filled her pockets with pony nuts. Misty was loaded and they were off.

Aunt Olwen drove. She said she knew exactly where the Spencers' house was. A friend of hers at the W.I. used to live in it.

* * *

The drive seemed to take forever. Mory thought they would never get there. She was longing to see Dancer and sat clutching the halter, putting it on Dancer again and again in her imagination. At last, Aunt Olwen turned the Landrover through a gate and up a smart gravel drive. Mr Spencer came out to greet them and waved them round the back. There was a small stable yard and beyond it a field where a black pony was grazing. It looked up as the trailer approached.

"It's Dancer!" cried Josh. Mory was too excited to speak.

Aunt Olwen backed the trailer into the yard and they climbed from the Landrover. Mr Spencer greeted the grown-ups.

"She's not a suitable pony at all for Caroline," Mory heard him say. "I had no idea there was so much to training these animals. She needs something much better than this."

"Mory," said Uncle Glyn, "go and bring Dancer in."

"I shouldn't let the child do it," said Mr Spencer. "It's vicious."

"Don't you think you should go with her, Glyn?" said Sheila.

"Let's see," said Uncle Glyn. "The pony's only been away from her a short while."

Mory ran to the gate. It had a proper pull-back handle which she found stiff, so she climbed it.

"Dancer!" she called. Dancer lifted her head and pricked her ears. Mory walked a few paces.

"Here, pony!" she called. Dancer let out a whinny of greeting and trotted to her. Mory held out some pony nuts. Dancer nuzzled Mory with her nose as she munched and Mory flung her arms around the pony's neck.

"You're mine now, Dancer! You're mine," said Mory into the pony's mane. Slipping Dancer's nose into the halter, she led her to the gate.

Mr Spencer took Mory's parents into the house. Uncle Glyn worked the stiff handle and the gate swung open. Laughing with happiness, Mory led Dancer to the trailer. Misty heard her hooves on the gravel and whinnied a greeting. Dancer whinnied a reply and walked up the ramp. Mory shared out all the pony nuts she had in her pockets. Dancer and Misty sniffed noses and pulled at the haynet Cara had tied up for them. The ramps were closed. Mory was itching to go in case Caroline Spencer changed her mind.

At last David and Sheila came out of the house. They shook hands with Mr Spencer and everyone piled into the Landrover.

"Well!" said Sheila. "You wouldn't know it was the same pony from what the Spencers say."

"It's all in the handling," said Uncle Glyn. "If frightened or upset she may have lashed out. We'll never know. Dancer seems all right and presumably the child has survived."

As they drove past the house Mory saw a face at a downstairs window. It was Caroline Spencer. For a moment Mory felt sorry for her, but only for a moment. She remembered that Mr Spencer was going to buy Caroline a better pony.

"Although no pony could be better than Dancer," thought Mory. "It's lucky they don't know that."

* * *

When they arrived back at Llangabby Mory led Dancer down the ramp. The pony looked enquiringly around to see where she was.

"Take the ponies down to Black Rock," said Uncle Glyn.

"Do you think Dancer will like Rustler?" asked Josh.

"You're about to find out," said Uncle Glyn.

The girls led the ponies down the track, Dancer walking eagerly along the path she knew so well. As they came into the yard at Black Rock Rustler whinnied a greeting. Josh opened the gate and Mory and Cara led the ponies in and let them go. Rustler sniffed noses briefly with Misty and wanted to know who the stranger was, then he sniffed noses with Dancer until she squealed and the three of them cantered off down the field. Dancer was delighted to be back and put in a fine buck.

Josh and Cara went back to Llangabby. They had a surprise birthday cake to make. Mory watched the ponies. She couldn't quite believe that Dancer was back. It was like the happy end to a story except, as she reminded herself, it was only the beginning. Once settled, Dancer must continue her training.

There was so much to do, so much to look forward to. Mory dragged herself away from the gate and went into the pottery. It was a shell with holes in the roof where David had begun taking off tiles. Soon her father would make pots in here and the more she helped, the sooner that would be. She was going to help him a lot. How exciting it all was!

Back in her room the three pictures of Dancer looked at her. With a whoop of sheer happiness Mory flung herself on the bed, kicking and waving her arms. Splodge fled to the safety of the landing.

"Everything's perfect!" she yelled at the top of her voice. "Do you hear that, Splodge? PURRFECT!" And she burst into a fit of giggles.

Three surprised pony faces looked towards the house, unused to such strange human sounds. But as nothing else happened to disturb them they quickly returned to the important business of eating.